The Zombiology Series

- The Reset (featured in: *Love At The End Of The World*)
- I Dream of Zombies
- The Six Million Dollar Zombies

But wait! There's still more stories to come in this world…

THE SIX MILLION DOLLAR ZOMBIE

A Zombiology Novel

Imogene Nix

2020 has been a hard year. For everyone.

It's also been a year of reflection, of completion and of learning about self and new things.

So I went to dedicate this book to anyone who learned a new skill, perfected an old one or just spent time with those closest to them.

Imogene Nix
2020

Contents

Chapter 1

Dove sighed and folded the vestments into the backpack. It wasn't quite how he'd ever expected to be living his life. If someone had told him three years ago that he'd be delivering sacraments using a lightweight motorbike to travel the countryside, rather like the traveling priests of old, he would have laughed.

"Hey, Dove! Are you coming?" The booming sound of Jamie's voice pulled him from his introspection.

"Yeah, just packing everything up now." The zipper made the ripping noise as it moved along the teeth, and he hefted the weight.

At least he was returning home today to the small house he inhabited, with the tiny chapel giving him space and privacy. Something he'd dreamed of during his time at Camp Queanbeyan.

Thank heavens for Julia. She'd seen him for who he was—a healer, medic, and priest. Not an executioner.

While he'd been seconded to her unit, he'd been able to give last rites to those they were putting to sleep, and he'd also been in the position of offering medical support to the team. She'd placed no label on him, unlike the camp commandant. The sour reminder of that time coated his tongue.

Jamie paced the floor outside the old, abandoned schoolhouse, his footsteps echoing loudly. The air was ripe with the scent of rotting fruit, withering on the vines, but Dove had seen another encampment of survivors who, while not thriving like the farm camp where he now lived, were finding a way to scrabble a life in a world that had changed dramatically. Most encampments were like that. Finding a hardscrabble life in the future they now inhabited post-zombie-apocalypse.

Jamie wheeled the bike out for him, and Dove slid on the orange helmet and waited for his guide, noting the heavy gauge weapon slung over his shoulder. These days most people went armed, in case of zombie attacks and other non-zombie opportunistic raids.

Until recently he too had carried a large cricket bat he'd found in one of their raids on the abandoned stores. With Jamie by his side, Julia had assured him, he'd be safe. She'd trained Jamie herself, along with her soon-to-be husband Leroy.

The throb of the machine after he'd ignited the engine filled the air, and the vibrations between his legs worked their customary magic. His body hardened, and he rolled his eyes, well aware there would be no sexual reprieve for him.

It wasn't that he was a sensual or even sexually experienced creature, but he did wish he could find a woman to love. A female to not just cherish but also open to him, so he could burn off the erection that made itself known. Unlike many of the other members of the camp, his beliefs didn't allow for casual hook-ups with the women who remained unpaired.

The air was crisp but not cold. The darkening of the sky as clouds rolled overhead and lightning flashing in the distance reminded him they had two hours back to the camp on the outskirts of what had been Canberra. The trees, skeletal branches reaching for the sky, shivered, moved by the rush of wind.

He glanced over his shoulder and noted the nod from Jamie. *Time to go.*

Dove gunned the machine, thankful for the heavy leather, weatherproofed suit they'd found for him last year, just before he'd taken on the visitations to the outlying settlements.

Liam, the camp's leader, had explained that he'd be able to

gather intelligence while traveling, share information and offer pastoral care. He could fulfill his calling, make alliances, and find out about the movements of the newly enhanced zombies. See where they were traveling to, and in what numbers.

The conspiracy, they now knew had started in the government ranks. The mess had run deep into the layers of government. The prime minister overthrown, the army inveigled into the plot, used to deliver the 'vaccines', which in turn had been found to be the carrier of the original infection, and millions of deaths ensued.

Those who'd been slated to deliver the second dose, the 'cure', had failed in their task and other governments had cut ties.

During Julia and Leroy's last mission, they'd all learned that a militia had been rounding up zombies and trucking them to a base. Where exactly, no one in their team of specialists had been able to ascertain, but they had managed to get their hands on a fresh specimen. The few remaining scientists had been busy looking for some kind of inoculation that would prevent further infection and hopefully even mutation.

They were battling waves of zombies, though the numbers were falling. At least, the ones who hadn't mutated.

He grunted as his bike jumped, riding over a stick embedded in the road. "Focus, Dove."

The engine of the bike whined, and not for the first time, he mourned the loss of radio stations. He'd enjoyed listening to the classics, but now silence filled the days as he rode.

Lightning split the sky, and on the road ahead, he caught sight of movement. A woman, ragged and filthy, limping in his direction.

Dove narrowed his gaze and eased up on the throttle. The sound of Jamie's engine doing the same let him know his guard and companion had also caught sight of her. They came to a stop several meters away.

"Help me!" Her pitiful cry and the wide-eyed terror shot slivers of ice through his gut.

He started to climb off the bike, but Jamie reached out a meaty hand and stopped him. "Wait," was all the big man muttered.

She came closer, her head turning to scan the road behind her. "Please, they'll catch me!"

The terror in her voice clawed at him. "Who?" he demanded.

"The… The zombies. They're coming this way." She turned back; tears etched a path down her cheeks. "Please. They've killed everyone else, and they're coming."

Now the dirge-like moaning filled the air, and she heaved, her face paling further under the slashing glare of the lightning.

He made a split-second decision. "Get on."

She shuffled slowly toward him, and Jamie growled, "We don't know who she is."

Her arms swept around him as she settled on the back end of the cushion—pillion, his mind helpfully added—and clutched tight.

In the distance he caught sight of the pack and grimaced. They'd taken too long.

"Go back to the camp then take the river road," he threw at Jamie as they revved the engines.

The bikes spun, spitting up gravel as the first heavy raindrops began to hit the ground with loud spatters.

LEONIE DIDN'T CARE who these men were. They had to be better than the zombies who had followed her from the vehicle. Or what remained of it.

Everyone else was gone, including her brother, and she was *alone*. Controlling the shiver of terror took everything, and for a moment, she nearly let go before sanity reasserted itself.

Surely it had to be divine intervention that brought these men right here and right now to save her? Leonie reached for the cross she'd worn until recently. Her hand came away empty. Just one more loss in a world that reeked of it.

The big man who didn't speak much had seemed unhappy with having her on the bike with the other guy. It didn't matter. They'd saved her from a fate that was infinitely worse than death.

They rode through the night, the wind wild and whipping at her dress, the ragged edges whacking her and tearing at her skin, while the cold rain pelted her. She was frozen to the core by the time they pulled into what she thought looked to be an abandoned house.

Sudden terror assailed. Why had they stopped here in the middle of nowhere? They couldn't have designs on her, could they? New fears raised their ugly heads the way zombies extended their grasping fingers.

"Why… Why are we…stopping here?" She couldn't control the broken cadence of her words nor the shivers which wracked her body. The cold, now bone deep, had her sure she'd shatter if she moved too quickly.

The man she was riding with gently dislodged her fingers, and she almost moaned as the heat of his skin scorched her.

"It's late, you're sodden and freezing. You're safe with us though. We will protect you."

He had no idea how much relief poured through her veins. Still… "But… We're not safe here, are we?" Leonie heard the threads of fear in her words.

The smaller man smiled, the blue of his gaze soft, as he cupped her face in his hands. "You need medical assistance, and we're not going to get back to the camp tonight with you like this. We need to wait for the worst of the storm to pass so we can see the road properly and anything in the way. Jamie will keep an eye out while I attend to you. We've got some food too. It looks like you could do with a meal or two." He spoke softly, as if soothing a wild animal.

She flinched. Food. Care. Comfort. Things she'd only dreamed of since the zombie invasion began.

"I'm thankful…"

The man smiled again, the corners of his eyes crinkling in the dimness. "I'm Dove."

Dove. The name felt like it fit him, if the softness and caring nature he appeared to exhibit was anything to go by. Tears pricked her eyes, and she scrubbed them away with the heels of her hands.

"I'm Leonie." She almost told him her siblings had called her Leo, but now that they were gone, she couldn't even begin to force those words past her stiff lips. Now her gut clenched hard. Gary, her brother, was gone. She'd seen what they'd done, the way they'd torn into the group in the vehicle, after they'd stopped because she just had to go to the bathroom.

Her fault. They'd only stopped because she'd demanded it. How could she live with that on her conscience?

Leonie bit her lip, feeling the bitter bile rising once again to burn her throat. Six souls, all lost because of her. The tears welled again, and she blinked, trying to clear them, but a black cloud enveloped her.

Shame. Guilt.

Why did I survive and not them? Why did Gary have to die?

Gary had heard of a camp he'd said weeks ago. Just today he'd said it wasn't far away and he had wanted them to get there today. It was big and safe. Welcoming to everyone, and their skills would be useful.

Gary was gone. She'd never again see his cheeky grin. Hear the long drawl as he ragged on her. There was no one else left from her family, and everything that connected them, biologically and physically, no longer remained. Struck down with the scourge of this terrible disease that ravaged Australia.

Leonie had to dig deep to remind herself she wasn't entirely alone and without assistance. Right in front of her stood a man, clearly gentle and caring if she was reading him correctly.

He steered her away from the door and tugged her down, so she settled on the bare board. He swung the large backpack he'd carried with him from his back. It had bitten into her stomach during the wild ride through the night, but she hadn't cared, because he'd saved her from the grasping fingers and sharp, biting teeth that tore and crunched.

God! The memory rose again. Scarlet blood spurting, white bone protruding, and the screams of terror…

Her stomach heaved, and she clapped her hand over her mouth, then moaned. "I'm going to be sick!"

Leonie scrabbled up, backed away from the man who followed her into what had once been a kitchen, and her hands gripped the dirty edges of the counter. He held her as she shook, her stomach heaving out its contents into the filthy metal of the sink.

Long moments passed as she squeezed her eyes shut, willing the roiling mass of her stomach to settle.

Afterward, Dove handed her a cloth and she wiped her mouth. Then he extended a water bottle, and she took it, swilling the bitter remnants from her mouth before greedily swallowing the contents.

He reached out, stilled her. "Slowly, or you'll be sick again."

Tears burned her eyes. "They're all dead, and it's my fault." Her voice broke, and he slid gentle arms around her as she shook.

"No. I doubt it's all your fault."

She shook her head, feeling the wet strands of hair slapping her face. Needing that little bite of pain, because every word she uttered was all true. "They stopped because I demanded it. I had to go to the toilet. Gary, my brother, was the driver, and he didn't want to, but I said…" Tears released like a torrent scorching her.

"Where were you going?"

She hiccupped and scrubbed at her eyes with the heels of her hand. "We'd heard of a farm, a little bit away from Canberra. A large but safe place is what we'd been told. We were headed for a small camp tonight along the way, then wanted to be at the farm where we'd heard there was safety. Gary was a mechanic, and he'd managed to get an old minivan going. We'd found it abandoned, and he'd siphoned every vehicle we passed."

"We?" Dove questioned, and she sighed.

"Gary and I had found some survivors over the last week we'd been on the road. We were coming in from the outback because there wasn't enough food or water at home." She flinched away from the memories of what lay behind her. There'd be time enough to share that later on, when she'd come to terms with what had gone before. "The drought is worsening, and we'd agreed that if we came closer to where others were, the food and water would last longer for those we left behind."

It was all true, but also far too late for Gary and the others she'd now left behind on a lonely road. He was the last of her family, and without him… A hand may as well have reached into her heart and squeezed the battered organ until it lay a ruin of bloodied muscle. The pain would be just the same, she was sure.

Leonie shook her head, desperately wishing she could dispel the memories of the sounds and the things she'd run from. The horror though stayed with her, a scar on her psyche.

Hiding in the tall grasses by the road, she'd been fine, hidden from the monsters until she'd screamed at the sights and atrocities unfolding before her. That was when they'd turned in her direction. En masse. They moved in her direction, quicker than a shamble, and some almost jogged toward her, so she'd done the only thing her brain demanded of her. *Run.*

Through the grass, into the thick bushes and trees she'd pelted. The stalks of the grass, sharp and hard, cut her legs while the branches tore her clothes. She lost a shoe somewhere along the way, but she didn't still to snatch it up. They were behind her, and the only safety was ahead, to run faster than them. Shoeless, the sharp stones cut her feet, but she kept going, as if the will and determination to survive had kicked in.

The zombies followed, the sounds of inhuman hunger freezing her innards. She couldn't say how long she'd run, at least an hour or more, before exhaustion nearly claimed her. Then she heard the engines, saw the motorbikes on the road ahead, outlined by the slash of lightning jagged in the sky, while wild winds and hard splotches of rain pelted her, and the wave of adrenaline that pushed her tired body forward gave out. She stilled, her brain unable to compute the sight before her.

"I just wanted to be safe," she whispered, broken inside at what she'd survived and witnessed. "Gary didn't care one way or another. He lost his wife and daughter to illness early on, but for me, he kept going. They hadn't come back as zombies, and I guess he'd been thankful for that. But me? I knew there was hope, Dove. We just needed to be safe. That's all. *Was it too much to ask?*" The cry came from the depths of her being.

She scrubbed her hands over her face. How could she possibly explain? She'd been a schoolteacher—a preschool instructor—in a small, private church school, where quiet and obedient has been the most important thing. She'd only left home long enough to gain her degree, then returned to the school where she herself had been educated. Her dream to educate, marry, and raise her own children likely dashed by the horror of the sickness sweeping Australia, and yet, she'd clung to hope until this.

He held her tight and rocked her, as if realizing how close to the edge she really was. "Shhh. It's okay. We'll take you to the farm. That's where we're from."

The words punched through her like spikes. Even in the midst of such horror, her hope had paid dividends again. "Thank you, God." She whispered the words quietly.

"Amen," Dove answered, and she started. Jumped out of his embrace to raise bewildered eyes to gaze upon him.

"Oh, I'm sorry. I meant to keep that to myself." It wasn't shame but embarrassment that warmed her cheeks.

His grin warmed her from the insides. "It's okay. I'm a believer." Something in the way he said the words, the way his grin deepened, tugged at something inside herself.

Once again, she raised her hand, seeking the tiny cross, then sighed. Gone. Like most other beloved items she'd ever owned.

"Oh. I'm pleased. It's…" She cleared her throat. "It's important to have something to hold onto these days." The wave of embarrassment crashed down on her as Leonie realized she was babbling. "Well, I'm warmer, and you've helped me a lot." Even more because he'd held her while she'd thrown up. *I don't want to remember that at all!*

"Before we go, let's clean up the scratches and pop some antibiotic ointment on them. Don't want to have an infection if we can avoid it."

"Would you…" She glanced away, embarrassed.

"What?"

"I hurt my foot too."

Holding the tattered edges of the dress so they didn't flop about, Leonie hobbled as she followed Dove back to the room. In his bag, there were wipes and ointments and a case.

She caught a flash of purple silk and her eyes darted to his. "So, uh what do you do?" Was he a priest? Or some kind of cross dresser? That flash of purple danced in her memory.

He smiled. "I'm a medic." He spoke quietly and his eyes darted away from hers, and she knew he wasn't telling her the truth, or at least not all of it.

"Oh. Okay then."

He set about checking her wounds then dug around in the bottom of the bag and tugged out a jumper and pair of long track pants. "They may be a bit big, but better than what you're wearing. I'll wrap your foot too, as I don't have any shoes."

Her eyes teared again. "Thank you."

After tending her feet, Dove left her to change, and she dove into the clothes, once more thanking the deity for helping her find safety, caring, and more hope.

It was only when she'd finished her hurried prayer the door slipped open and Jamie stuck his head around the corner. "Rain's gone. We better go."

⸻

DOVE ADJUSTED his backpack onto his chest. It would make for an uncomfortable ride, but he'd made his decision to take the girl with him. Jamie had offered to carry his pack for him, but with the contents becoming pretty damn close to irreplaceable, he preferred to look after them himself.

The girl—Leonie—climbed on behind him, her fingers winding tight around his waist. It had been years since he'd felt the grip of a woman like this. His mind wound back to Marci Hines, the girl he'd left behind when he'd joined Seminary. Not that either of them had engaged in more than mutual groping and hot kisses. Even then, he'd known where his future lay—in the church—and even though he wasn't Catholic, meaning he could choose to marry, he'd understood that physical lovemaking should be constrained to marriage. It was one of the aspects of the religious life he found somewhat constraining at times.

Shaking his head, he cleared the wooliness, allowing him to think clearly once more. Walking around in his memories would be reserved for when they were safely home on the farm. It was far too dangerous to lose concentration on the roads with zombies hanging around looking for an easy mark.

"Everything okay?" a small voice asked behind him.

He inhaled deeply. "Yeah. Ready?"

Jamie gave him the signal to move, and they roared out onto the road, which was pitted with grasses thrusting up between the gravel. Nature reclaims all, he thought whimsically, sliding around a larger tuft. He and Jamie stayed side by side, the wheels spinning quickly as they headed for home.

The closer they came to Canberra, the more wrecks they passed. He could tell that Leonie was startled each time because her nails caught on his jacket and dug in. More than once he slowed, worried she might fall off the back of the bike if they jolted hard, but she stuck the distance.

His eyes kept returning to the gas needle, hoping they had enough, with the extra passenger. He knew Jamie said if they went a little slower than usual, they should be okay, but it was only when the fence around their camp loomed that he could relax. *We made it.*

The gates opened and in they rode.

Not for the first time, he felt pride in what they were building here. A community of civilians, though many doubled up as guards. Liam and Elaine, the camp's leaders, had been insistent that the majority of residents should take turns, and the young should be trained to keep them safe. The future of the community relied on everyone pulling their weight.

They were more than a military outpost with a school, hospital, and farm. This was a home, where everyone was welcome. Including him.

The gates closed behind them, and Jamie, Leonie, and himself climbed from the bikes.

Liam wandered out, scrubbing his hand through his hair and a damp white patch on his shoulder. "You've brought a visitor with you?"

"A new member," explained Dove.

Liam smiled and extended a hand to the woman whose fingers twisted in the long sleeves of his jumper. "Okay, how about you two come in. Jamie, go grab something to eat, and you can fill me in on what you learned later." Then Liam patted the man on the shoulder before Jamie lumbered off to the large shed that had become the main dining hall.

They both trailed Liam inside, Leonie following slowly while Dove brought up the rear. They moved quietly through the kitchen and into the small lounge. It still gave Dove pause to see a 'normal' suburban home in the middle of such chaotic times.

"Elaine's asleep. She had a bad night with Isla." Liam's wife had recently given birth to their first child.

"They're both doing well?" Dove asked.

"Yeah, but Isla's not settling well. I'm going to ask Ramon for advice. Elaine's exhausted and worried." Liam sat down in the chair, and Leonie and himself plonked themselves down.

"Does she still want me to baptize the baby?"

Liam grinned at Dove. "You know we do. Just need to arrange some time for that."

Dove noted the shocked look on Leonie's face. "Baptize?"

He sighed. "Before all this, I was a priest. I'm still a medic and assist when I'm needed on a mission, but..." Dove shrugged. Not everyone believed, and too many found their faith tested these days. He hadn't lied, just hadn't told her everything until now. It always sat badly hiding what else he was, but that was a learned behavior from his time at Camp Queanbeyan.

Now, Dove focused on Liam again, marshalling his thoughts. "Leonie here was on the road. Running from zombies. The car she and her brother and a group were traveling in were overwhelmed when they stopped for a relief break. She escaped, but the others didn't. She saw it all, then ran." Dove spoke quietly, hoping she'd be able to explain the rest of what occurred without breaking down in tears.

He'd attended many of these discussions, knowing Liam understood that sometimes the presence of a priest soothed those who suffered guilt and survivor's syndrome. While he wasn't a counselor, he was the only one at this stage who had any training in dealing with traumatic events.

She sighed and held herself still. His impression was she was as brittle right now as old glass, fragile, and it would only take an unwary move and she would shatter. "My brother Gary and I were traveling in from the outback. The town we came from has about ninety people left, but with the drought, the water supplies are running low." She shrugged when Liam made a sound. "We decided that if we left, it might let the supplies last a little longer. Anyway, we headed for the coast. On the way, we stopped to siphon vehicles, picked up those who wanted to come with us. We'd been traveling for a couple of weeks. Going slowly makes the petrol go further, Gary says. He's..." Her voice broke and she shook. Her face scrunched up tight, as if she were holding onto her emotions.

Dove reached out and touched her shoulder. "It's okay. We understand."

She nodded and gave a hiccupping sigh. "It was my fault. We stopped because I had to go to the bathroom. We'd been traveling for a couple of hours, and I... I was in the grass, you know, when they came. There were lots. Big and loud. They surrounded the vehicle, and I heard them. Couldn't look away. They broke through the glass. Gary screamed at me. Said *run*, but I couldn't. But I saw it all. Inside the minivan they were trapped. The zombies..." Her hand snaked out and latched onto Dove's.

Liam rose and disappeared into the kitchen, returning quickly with a glass of water.

She took the drink and gulped, then sat there, frozen with the glass in her hand, distance in her green eyes.

"They're all dead?" Liam's quiet question broke the silence.

"Yes." With shaking hands, Leonie slid the glass to the small coffee table between the chairs.

"You ran?" prompted Dove.

"Yes. Through the grass and the trees. They followed me after I screamed. Just followed me, and I was terrified. That's when I ran into—"

"Dove and Jamie," added Liam.

Leonie nodded.

Liam's gaze turned to Dove. "Did you see them?"

Dove shook his head. "No, but we heard them. They're slower moving than the mutates, so I'm guessing these aren't the newer species. We turned and came back via the alternate route. We didn't see any on the roads at all." He hoped Leonie had missed the references to the mutation. She was traumatized enough right now, and adding to it? Well, he refused to do that as the sudden, and surprising, sense of protectiveness rose inside him.

Liam considered Dove and Leonie's report with a frown. "None on the roads at all? That's odd. There's usually some, so I wonder if that means—"

"They've rounded them all up?" a tired female voice echoed from the stairs behind him.

Dove turned to see Elaine, a tiny baby over her shoulder as she entered the room. With the ease of familiarity, Elaine passed the baby to Liam then bustled into the kitchen before returning moments later with a cup of tea in her hand. She settled on the last seat of the old couch.

"Seems to me the zombie collection has ramped up, and whether that means they're doing well, or their experiments are a failure, neither scenario is great," Elaine said.

The baby started to fuss, and Leonie sighed. "I just adore babies." She reached out a hand, then snatched it back. "Sorry, back home everyone would get a nurse, but the babies are all gone." Her face turned bleak. "We couldn't get baby food, so the mayor had them and their families moved to somewhere they would be safe at the beginning of things. That only left the single and older adults and teens behind to work the properties." Now when she turned to Liam it was a sad and weary look that filled her eyes. "Gary was the town's only mechanic and general dogsbody. He was useful, but my job…" She shrugged. "Well, without any little kids, I wasn't very useful. For a while I grew veggies, but I think I've got a brown thumb."

Elaine reached for a notebook. "So, what do you do?"

"Oh, I'm a preschool teacher. Anything from birth to six years really is where my talents are best used." Leonie sounded so woebegone that Dove wanted to fold her in his arms. He had to hold himself very tightly to ward off that instinctual move.

Elaine's eyes lit up. "Well, that's great because we have lots of youngsters here, and while we have a creche, it's in need of some direction. But let me get some basic information from you."

Elaine noted down her name—Leonie Jane Manners—and where she'd been born. Her age and marital status.

"We'll get the rest later, when you get a chance to meet with Julia. First, we'll get you settled in the newcomer's quarters. You'll need to see Ramon, our resident doctor, for a physical exam."

Leonie reached out, grabbing onto Dove's hand. "But… I don't know anyone and…" Terror and shock were clearly foremost in her mind as Leonie shook. Her breath came in pants, and Dove knew she was about to have a panic attack.

He patted her hand, and she turned, giving him her full attention. "I've got a spare room at my place. She can stay there."

Liam's eyes widened. Elaine simply stared.

"She'll be safe there, and perhaps being around someone she already feels comfortable with will help her assimilate quicker." Dove didn't examine why he'd made the offer.

"Sure. If you're both comfortable with that? We can look for singles accommodation later on, when you're ready," soothed Elaine, and Liam nodded in agreement. "Go grab some food, and don't forget to take Leonie to see Julia tomorrow, so we can note the who's and where's for the census."

They rose, and Dove showed Leonie to the door, aware that she'd snaked her hand into his grip.

He had to ward off the sensation of warmth. He was a priest, he reminded himself. There to give comfort and support, not to take them from her.

Chapter 2

Leonie couldn't say why she felt so comfortable and safe with Dove. It could be that he simply showed her where to be, made sure she'd eaten, and shared his home with her—for the meantime anyway.

It might be that once she'd worked out what he was—a *priest*—she felt he'd have no interest in her and wouldn't demand the intimacy of a romantic connection between them.

Bah humbug!

Maybe it was because he made no moves while she was still struggling to come to terms with Gary's death? Then again, Leonie also knew that her thoughts might just be colored by the information she didn't tell Liam and Elaine. The underlying reason of why they'd had to leave town to escape what the mayor had in mind for her, or that the world as she knew it ceased to exist.

The knowledge of the secrets she kept littered her mind and preoccupied her as Dove took her to the shed containing the clothing stores. There she gratefully accepted packets of bras and panties, shirts and pants, shoes, and even toiletries.

Many of the shampoos and cleansers appeared home-made, and when she asked, the girl manning the desk grinned. "We have a couple of people here who make all the cosmetics and skin care products."

A toothbrush, hairbrush, and even hair bands added to the pile, and soon, she had archiving boxes filled to the brim.

"Do you need any medications?" Dove spoke quietly behind her, and she jumped, almost having forgot him for a moment.

Leonie turned to him and grinned, his arms full of bedding and the necessary linens for another person. "No. I'm actually really healthy, I think."

"Okay, so we'll go back to my place and you can take a few minutes to put your stuff away, then we'll go over and see Ramon. He's Liam's brother. A little terse but a great physician. It's lucky he and Liam were here when the outbreak started."

Leonie shook her head. "Here? What do you mean?"

"From what I understand, this was Elaine's grandmother's place, and Liam and Ramon were here on holidays or something. It was Liam and Elaine who rounded up the neighbors and formed the first community, then Ramon joined them when they closed the nearby hospital. The community expanded over time, and there's also a couple of satellite communities now as well as a reclaimed resort over there." Dove waved his hand in the direction of 'out there.' "They couldn't keep everyone safe in the original patches, which includes the school and houses around here. The resort houses singles who come and go daily, with increased security."

"O-kay." The amount of organization they'd achieved in a couple of years was overwhelming. Besides which, some of the conversation between Elaine, Liam, and Dove had pricked her interest. "But what were they saying about mutations back there?"

"Look, let's get back to the house and I'll explain over a coffee. Does that work for you?"

Coffee? "You have coffee?" The words escaped as an excited squeak.

"Carefully rationed, yes, but we do. And even better, we've got trees we relocated from a plant store. Actually, lots of the plants we grow now are 'reclaimed.' The farm has cows, sheep, and pigs.

We've got chickens and grow our own vegetables. We have a couple of women who have taken over control for preserving the produce too."

Leonie bit her lip. "What about water?" It was one of the largest issues back home. It was the reason things had taken the turn they did. The curdling sensation in her belly when she remembered made itself known again.

"We have a bore, which was harnessed early on, I think. Then we have solar power and mechanics and engineers. They're teaching some of the youngsters now, so when they retire, we have someone ready to take over. We even have a sewerage system. It's rudimentary but works okay for now."

Is this some kind of heaven in the middle of hell?

He ushered her into a small building that looked like a converted shed. The outer walls of bare corrugate though inside was paneled and painted. He'd made some effort with a cheery fireplace in a corner and big throw on the floor. She blinked as they entered the tiny house in the rear, a tidy kitchen and lounge with three doors leading off it.

"That's my room, the bathroom, and this one…" He nudged the door open and sighed, noting the piles of washing on the unmade bed. "This will be yours. I'll just grab my stuff and here's your sheets and pillows."

The normality of it struck her as silly, and a tiny laugh bubbled up from her belly. It rolled and grew bigger, and she dropped the boxes she held as hysteria took root.

Dove cursed, dropped the bedding on the tiny two-seater lounge, and dragged her close. "It's okay to cry. It's okay to not feel okay. Just let it out, Leonie."

And she did. The high-pitched laughter turning into hacking sobs that tore her body. It was noisy but also therapeutic to let go. Leonie dug her fingers into the sinews of his shoulders and clung hard.

Afterward, she felt spent. Exhausted.

"I'm sorry. I shouldn't have—"

"Shhh… You've been through a lot. We all understand these things. Now come on. If you want to wash your face, I'll clear my washing, then we'll have a drink of tea or something else, given I take it, you're a coffee drinker?"

"Oh, coffee, please," she mumbled and headed for the bathroom.

It was small and compact. A toilet, small sink, and shower, but he'd told her the water was running. That also meant the toilet flushed. It was far more than she'd had in the last year or two. Leonie made short work of washing up, cleaning her face and arms as best as she could and gazing now and then at the shower stall.

He had a steaming brew waiting on the counter as she entered the lounge. Embarrassment burned her face, waves of heat radiating as she saw him. For the first time, she wondered how this had come to be. She was exactly where she and Gary—and man, did the grief punch hard now, though she restrained it— had planned to be. She was living with the world's best looking priest. *What a waste!*

He wasn't a giant. A little taller than her height, and his hair dark as midnight. His eyes a dark gray-blue that reminded her of storm clouds. Stubble dotted his jawline, yet through the dark, she noted the hard edges of his chin. He'd shed his jacket and stood there in a black shirt and jeans with the white of his clerical collar showing.

"Umm, what kind of priest are you?" Leonie closed her eyes at the banality of her question. *God, what an idiotic thing to ask!*

He laughed. "What kind do you think I am?"

She bit her lip. In the midst of all this mess, she found him *attractive.*

Bad Leonie! Bad! He's a sodding priest, not a potential boyfriend.

"I don't know." Then, because she really wasn't sure she wanted to know the answer, she changed tacks. "But how do you cope with all this around you? The literature I got with my clothes, which had the rules of the camp on it, said we'd have to have kids."

He winced. "Yes. We'll need to think about replacing ourselves so later on we can continue to work the camp."

"Never mind," she muttered, feeling all kinds of stupid. After all, what the hell was she thinking? Priests didn't get married, because they dedicated themselves to the work of the church.

"No, it's okay. At some point I'll get married too. Hopefully have kids."

His words set off a chain reaction in her belly. Married. Kids. *"But you're a priest!"*

He laughed, the sound filling the air again, and her belly wobbled. "An Anglican priest. We marry. It's not breaking our faith."

Leonie formed an 'o' with her mouth. She should have paid more attention to the non-Catholic faith growing up.

"My role here is priest, counselor, spiritual guide. I'm also on the community board and help in the gardens. From time to time I assist with the hospital and work in the school. My talents are varied." He listed his tasks easily and took a sip of his drink. "I'm also a dab hand in the kitchen, which leads me to what would you like to eat? It's sort of late for breakfast but early for lunch. I'm hungry, and I bet you are too."

Leonie's stomach growled, and she winced. "I don't know. It's been a long time since I've had a cooked meal. Along the way we found old cans of food and ate them when we siphoned fuel. What have you got?"

He listed some options and she made a choice.

She inhaled as he moved around the kitchen, clearly at ease. "I saw a group as we arrived going out. Are they some kind of guides?"

"No, Liam still sends teams out looking for things that will be useful to the camp. We've emptied most of the schools hereabouts of the things we can use, like readers and writing books. The pharmacies were emptied earlier by Ramon and his crew. We're always on the lookout for clothing and low-tech transport options. Last month, the team brought home about a hundred and fifty bikes they'd found in an old department store."

She gaped. It all seemed like a dream. "I can't..." Leonie shook her head.

He grinned and opened a cupboard near his legs. "What kind of milk do you prefer with your corn flakes?"

"Real milk?" Her stomach growled again, and the thought of a 'normal' breakfast beckoned.

"Yeah."

A bubble of laughter, this time real, escaped. "That sounds like heaven."

DOVE WONDERED ABOUT LEONIE. Her face was clean though her hair had matted. From Elaine's questions and Leonie's answers, he knew she was in her mid-twenties. She and her brother had set out on a dangerous journey together.

It begged the question, why had no one else from their township come with them? She'd already shared the lack of water, but if that was the case, why not travel in a convoy from the start?

Liam would want to know more about her situation and where she'd come from, but Dove had an inkling that her story and scars were much more involved than the skim of details she'd shared. What would they find when she told everything she knew?

Instead of trying to pick out facts based on guesswork, he focused on watching her eat. She didn't wolf through the food, instead took slow and deliberate spoonfuls, chewing carefully, and from time to time closing her eyes, as if savoring flavors long missed.

When she finished Leonie sat there, eyes still closed. "That's the best meal I've had in so long."

"What did you eat at home?"

Leonie grimaced and opened her eyes. "All the food was stock-piled. Anything we had had to be shared, though I don't think that's a bad thing. What got me is some people had better shares than others. When things got tough, we shot the birds from the sky. The worst was the eagles, 'cause they're old and stringy." Leonie pulled a face. "And wormy."

He waited, knowing she'd have to tell him what she could in her own time.

"Then the mayor had a bright idea. He decided he wanted a wife and rounded up all the females of the 'right' age." Leonie made brackets in the air with her fingers. "Said continuation meant we had to reproduce. A couple of girls refused, and he banished them from the town." Leonie turned her face away from him.

A flame of fury shot to life in Dove's gut. He was pretty sure he knew what came next. "They were found?"

"A couple of weeks later, the birds were circling in the distance. A group of guys went out. Found Lana and Jane. They'd died of starvation and dehydration, they think." She glanced back at Dove, her eyes glistening with tears and remembered fear. "He sent them away knowing they had to walk. He wouldn't even give them a gun to protect themselves." Her voice was thick with unshed tears and fury. "The nearest town was hundreds of kilometers away. He didn't care. That's when the men told him no more banishments. The women weren't there just for him to perpetuate his family. They kept him under arrest for a couple of weeks, but he was the mayor. When they released him, he just resumed what he'd done before."

"He chose you?" Dove's fingers clenched and the well of lava hot fury burned his guts.

"Not right away. He picked Lana's little sister, Carla. She was willing enough, and they married. She got pregnant, but something went wrong. The baby got stuck, and the nurse in town, she tried to deliver it. They didn't know the cord was wrapped around its throat. Carla finally delivered it after a couple of days, but she hemor-rhaged from the birth. Died that evening. After that, things got really bad." Leonie dropped her head, rubbed her brow.

Then things got really bad? How much worse could it be?

He clenched his fists, containing himself with difficulty, because on her face he read the emotional scars she carried in the fragile way she held herself. He wondered how deep the trauma ran.

"Gary kept me inside as much as he could, to keep me out of his way. He'd take me out with him if he had to work on something on a property. He wouldn't leave me at home alone. Then recently the mayor decided I might be an option. Came around a lot and finally told me what he planned. Gary said we had to go, and to be honest,

I was pretty pleased to get out of there. So, we did. Only took a few things…" Now tears dribbled down Leonie's cheeks again. "I lost them all. The photos. Gary."

Dove stood and shuffled around to the other side of the bench. She scooted closer as if needing the reassurance of human touch, yet afraid to allow the intimacy.

"We've all lost a lot, Leonie. It hurts, and it sucks. I can't promise anything, but maybe the next time I'm out that way, we can look. If we see the van, we'll try to retrieve the photos. If you want us to?"

"I… I think I'd like that, but what if Gary is…"

He knew exactly what she was asking. "Jamie knows what to do. I can give absolution and a final blessing if it makes you feel better?"

She bit her lip, clearly torn by the reality that if her brother had transformed, they'd have to deal with him, yet wanting those reminders of a life long gone. He wanted to give her peace of mind, but he couldn't and wouldn't lie. Not to her or anyone else. There was no easy way to deal with the realities of their new life.

"How about a shower? Then I can take you over to see Julia. She'll be in her office. I have to check in with the hospital, and I can make an appointment for you with Ramon and start the process of organizing a work detail for you. You can also pop into the library if you want. It's rudimentary, but there's at least a range of books. We're stuck for space, so while there are more, we just don't have any way to keep them organized."

Leonie brightened at his suggestions. "Sure, but um, I need to find some clean clothes and…" She looked down at his trackpants and sweater top. "These were fine, but I'd like to have my own clothes, if that's okay?"

"Sure. Grab what you want and head into the bathroom, I'll clear all my stuff out, and by the time you're done, we'll be ready to head over to the census office."

He waited until she'd rummaged through her boxes, keeping his gaze averted. After all, what girl wanted an unknown guy watching her find her underwear? She'd been embarrassed enough when she'd grabbed what she'd needed from the store, and he didn't intend to make things worse.

He grabbed the piles of washing and books he'd dumped on the single bed and shuffled them to his room, keeping his door open in case she needed something. The books he shoved onto the bookcase, then sorted his clothes, folded and stuffed them into the drawers he'd claimed for his room.

"I should wash more often," he muttered. From the pile of items he grabbed a packet of pillows, a blanket, and some sheets.

"I could do that for you, if you like. I enjoy washing."

Her words startled him, and he turned, suddenly shocked at the pretty woman who stood in his doorway. Her hair now brushed, hung in damp curls, framing her pale face. Her fine skin was porcelain clear, and long lashes circled her green eyes. She'd dressed in shorts and a t-shirt, her feet encased in white sneakers with tiny white socks. Long, shapely legs tapered up to her knees before disappearing beneath the hem of the denim shorts.

It took a moment to recapture the thread of what she'd said, his mind fogged with a sudden urge to know her better. "I um… I don't like washing."

She laughed. "I gathered that." The mirth fled and she blinked. "Uh, what would you like me to call you? Father or—"

Now he sputtered. "I'm not old."

She blushed. "Oh, I didn't mean to embarrass you. I just meant…"

He sighed, aware that a distance forced by his vocation had opened between them. "It's okay. Everyone hereabouts, except some of the older ladies, call me Dove."

"Is that you real name?" Leonie asked.

"No. Well, not exactly. My full name is Dov Caleb. My parents loved the Hebrew names, and Dov is…well, Hebrew. It means bear. Anyway, everyone pronounced it Dove, and it just stuck. So, I answer to it."

"Wow, my name is Leonie because Mum liked this actress in a television show. Mum and Dad were big television watchers. All the kids were named after them." Her voice trailed off. "Well, I guess we better get on with meeting this Julia."

She'd changed the subject, likely hoping to shut down discussion and memories of the past. He wanted to tell her that it wasn't healthy, but he knew meeting with Julia would be difficult enough, so he let it ride. For now.

Chapter 3

Leonie entered the building, another shed construction, and inside there was a single tiny room where Julia waited. The room was cluttered, with two desks, a couple of old computers, a large duplexing printer, and filing cabinets. Dove rubbed her shoulder as if he knew her nerves were jumping inside her.

"When you're done, Julia will walk you back to my house. Make yourself comfortable when you get back there. I shouldn't be too long."

She watched Dove walk away and felt like a tiny chink of herself left with him. It was an oddly disquieting feeling and something she'd never before experienced. The woman in the seat with the old computer in front of her smiled, in a kind way. Her hair was short, giving her a pixie-like look, except for the piercing quality of her gaze.

"I'm Julia. Welcome to our Births, Deaths, Marriages, and Census hut. Make yourself comfy." She gestured toward a padded seat and Leonie sat down. "You're staying with Dove?" Julia cocked her head to one side as if expecting some kind of answer.

"Yes. I'm not…" Leonie floundered, lost for words to describe how *at ease* she was with Dove. Something about him reassured her on an instinctual level. It was deeper than the fact he'd saved her. Why, she couldn't quite tease out just yet, but that was the unvarnished truth.

"He's a great guy and will make sure you're okay before you're allocated a place in the singles housing units." Julia smiled and reached for a book, scooping up a pencil. "Okay, I need some basic details to start your file. Your full name, date and place of birth, and parents' names first."

Julia asked questions, and Leonie answered them as fully as she could. Some of them, like the ones about the death of her parents, Gary, and sister Jenna hurt. *A lot.* It seemed like she had to wade through lots of things that hurt before she could embrace the good stuff that was in her future, though right now it didn't seem either fair or reasonable to suffer further.

When they were done, Leonie was emotionally exhausted, and her eyes burned. In one hand she clutched a handkerchief Julia had given her from a stash she kept in her drawer.

"It must be hard dealing with people who are coming to terms with so much loss," Leonie muttered.

Julia's eyes darkened. "Sometimes it is," she admitted, her voice low. "But we can honor their memory. That's what makes this so important. Plus, sometimes there are opportunities to reunite members of a family."

Julia practically bounced in her seat, her eyes widening and bright, and a big smile bloomed on her face.

"I had one last month. The mother and daughter were at another location. They were looking for the father, who was here. It was only when we sent a request out to the other camps that we found they were all still alive. That was a hell of a reunion, and we celebrated well into the next day. It doesn't happen often, but that we might be able to help, makes it all worth the hours and pain, Leonie. And when we can't do that, then we can remember them on our remembrance tree. You should ask Dove about that, when you're ready. Now, do you want to head right back or would you like to check out—"

"Umm, Dove mentioned a library. Could you show me where it is?"

Julia grinned. "Sure, let me grab my books that need returning and I'll take you over there. We'll get you issued a borrowing card and see if there's something that appeals."

DOVE SIGHED HEAVILY and wiped his brow. What was Leonie doing now? In his mind, he pictured her face strained and Julia offering sympathy.

Julia was good at that, teasing out the information that would allow her to concoct a brief family history for the records. He supposed it was because it's what she'd done before the apocalypse. His mind returned to Leonie. Was she doing okay?

He snorted. "She'll be fine. She's come this far and has a spine, Dove."

He thrust the shovel back into the dirt, having agreed to help plant some of the new vegetables in exchange for a bag of potatoes, pumpkin, carrots, beans, and beef. He made a mean steak and veggies and thought it had probably been a long time since Leonie had a meal like that. He took feeding his houseguest very seriously.

The hole dug, he carefully placed the implement aside and crouched next to the last chard, crumbling the toilet paper roll from around the roots and sliding it into the dirt. Then he backfilled the dirt around the new plant and watered it.

Rows of vegetables, healthy and green, met his gaze. If it weren't for the losses they'd all incurred, he could almost think he was in a gentler world.

He rose and picked up the discarded shovel and watering can and headed for the hut at the far end of the field. One of the supervisors offered a cloth, and Dove wiped off the shovel and handed it to the man waiting, then walked toward the stores.

The bags of food were lined up, and he accepted it gratefully before heading for his house. A glance at the sky told him the day wasn't yet over, so likely Julia still had Leonie occupied.

Dove told himself he'd slip into the house and shower and dress ahead of her arrival home. Perhaps he'd have the meal cooking already by the time she walked through the door? Satisfaction at that plan welled, and he entered the house. All was quiet so he took off his shoes at the door, frowning at the dirt caked on them, then he headed for the tiny kitchen zone.

After sliding the food into the refrigerator, he stepped into the bedroom to retrieve some clothes. Jeans and a fresh shirt, some underwear, and he was ready.

At the bathroom door, feeling a bit like a fool, he knocked. As there was no answer he wandered in then stopped short. Signs of Leonie lay on the tiny washstand. A brush, toothbrush, and basic skin care items.

The sight of them reminded him that his life was changing. It was as if her safety and happiness were his responsibility, and made greater by a bond which existed between them. With a sigh, he closed the door and latched it, divested himself of the dirty clothes, and stepped into the shower.

The feel of warm water sluicing over his skin refreshed and invigorated him, and he welcomed the feeling. When he stepped from the shower and toweled off, he appreciated the clean clothes as if he were ready for anything. As he hung up his towel, Dove couldn't help but notice hers hanging on the rack beside it.

Opening the door, he started at seeing Leonie in the kitchen, a pot on the stove and the scent of frying meat filling the air.

"Oh, I hope you don't mind. I found some food in the freezer and started cooking. It's been so long since I've had the opportunity to cook a proper meal." Leonie's gaze was surprised and a little chagrined, as if she'd been caught in some kind of plot.

Dove may have planned to cook for her, but this was just as welcome, and he could cook the steaks tomorrow night, he guessed. "What's for dinner?" he quipped.

She blushed. "Spaghetti and meatballs?"

His stomach gurgled its approval. "Sounds great. Haven't had that in a long time. What do you want me to do?"

"Well, you could lay the table and get some of those bread slices, foil, and herbs, and we can make some garlic butter."

He was liking the sound of her dinner more and more. "Sure. I've also got some cheese one of the ladies made, so we can have that, or I think there may be a can of dry parmesan in the cupboard."

Before he even finished the words, she held it up for him to see.

"I was excited when I found the fresh herbs in the garden. They really set you up properly, don't they?" Leonie turned back to the stove, stirring the rich tomato sauce, her hair tied back though tendrils had escaped the confines and framed her face.

"They raided the shops and houses, and while some things are in short supply, they try to give us most of the basics so we can continue to live a semi-normal life."

She stilled at the stove while Dove watched. "It's crazy, isn't it? I mean zombies. No one ever thought they would really be…real. I wonder how it came about?" she mused.

The question soured his stomach, because he knew the answer. Hell, most of the camp did these days. It wasn't exactly a secret, but still, how did he tell Leonie? He cleared his throat, marshalled his thoughts, and dove on in.

"It was a plot that went wrong. Factions of the government that went too far. They released the live virus into the water system, meaning to inoculate against it, but it didn't work the way they planned. There's also another group that's rounding up zombies and attempting to mutate the virus."

She gasped and stepped away from the stove, wooden spoon in her hand and sauce dripping down. "You *are* joking, right?" Her eyes were wide with shock. "No one in their right mind would do something like that."

Dove shook his head. Memories of the wild mission to retrieve the hand—because a sample had been required to prepare a vaccine; one which was unsuccessful—rushed into his mind. As much as he might want to forget, they were now part of him. Along with what came after.

"Anyway, we're safe here. This was one of the first camps set up, and one of the best organized. There are rosters and responsibilities, but everyone accepts that they must do their bit. Our water system is carefully controlled and is one of the reasons we've managed to grow and flourish."

"But you said—" Her eyes rounded, and she paled. Swayed before shooting out a hand and gripping onto the benchtop.

Was she going to faint?

One careless utterance had brought her close to meltdown.

Dove shook his head. "It's a case of some were given a role they didn't understand. One of the men is here, he's not just remorseful for what he did, but is doing good things to help us. He's got what I believe is PTSD from his actions—"

"*Here?*" Her tone rose with a negative emotion. "Among those who had nothing to do with—" Fury replaced the shock on her face, and she dropped the spoon into the pot with an agitated jerk.

"Yes. In his defense, he was following orders and didn't know what he was working with. He's a good man. A friend of mine." He tried to calm her, explaining the situation, but felt like it was careening out of control.

Now he rounded the bench, took her shoulders, and noted the width of her pupils and the heightening of her exhalations. *Shock.* He needed to do something quickly.

He steered her to a seat, pushing her down and crouching in front of her. "We—all of us—have done things that weren't good, Leonie. Things that didn't sit well with our consciences."

How did he make her understand that Leroy—Julia's partner—had been acting purely under orders? That he was a good man who'd done something heinous without realizing the ramifications of following orders at the time? That he genuinely needed to make up for it and suffered daily with the knowledge?

"Hey, listen to me."

Her gaze settled on him. "You've never done anything wrong though. You're a priest." Her voice was thready, and she reached out, clutching his hands.

His laugh was tight. "I'm not a saint. I've done wrong, and things that are gray even. Since we've been here, I've compromised my beliefs for the greater good. Not because I believe in it, but because to send others who are totally unprepared into the fray wouldn't be right or even borderline acceptable. Sometimes, the greater good is more necessary than protecting ourselves."

She blinked. "Like what?"

A hard question, and one he wished he could avoid. "I can't talk about it right now, okay? I…" God, he wanted to shy away from this question, the memories of what he'd done. The things he had to live with and atone for. "There was a mission," he merely told her. "The information I was able to bring back helped us immensely."

Leonie reached up and cupped his face, her gaze softening. He detected the first trace of understanding in her that he was human. A man. That he was no saint, but red-blooded.

The knowledge ricocheted through him, spearing his mind.

"Dove?" She whispered his name. Seeking more.

He shook his head, unwilling to discuss it. "It was a mission for Liam and Elaine. Gathering information. Please, no more tonight. Be aware, Leroy will be visiting sometime soon, and I'd really like you to be open to the knowledge that he's human and in pain. Okay?"

Her lips thinned, but she gave a slow nod. "I'll try, Dove. For you, okay?"

THE EVENING DRAGGED BY SLOWLY. After the pre-dinner discussions about how the zombie infection had been spread, Leonie had finished cooking, though the meal was quiet. She'd been trying to come to terms with what Dove had told her and he'd let her be.

Then Dove took over the cleaning up and encouraged her to settle down comfortably with the book she'd borrowed from the library. It was one she'd read before—a classic romance—and as much a reinforcement that her life had once again dramatically changed, but it appeared for the better this time. It also allowed her to escape for a short while back to the kind of life she'd dreamed of having.

Dove settled beside her, his hands full of sheets of paper that apparently held something amusing, because he smiled and occasionally chuckled. A sound she hadn't heard in such a long time. Gary had always been busy, and when he hadn't, he'd been planning where they'd go or grieving the loss of his wife and young daughter. Smiles, laughter, and good times had been in short supply for the last couple of years, and she eyed Dove over the edge of the pages each time the sound pealed.

Dove was a strange man, for a priest. Good looking, straight talking, and young. Well, younger than all the others she'd had anything to do with, she mused. Obviously, they started out younger before migrating to the western areas, or at least that had been her experience in the local Catholic church. The knowledge was distinctly unsettling in so many ways.

He'd spoken rather sternly to her when explaining that Leroy, an ex-soldier, had been given the role of placing the initial live virus in a water supply chosen by his superiors. She wasn't sure that it in any way absolved him as yet.

She didn't know anything much about him except the reality of what he'd done and that he was partnered with Julia of the Births, Death, and Marriages hut. What Dove's words did do though was etch away at the narrow band of black and white as she saw it, because she trusted him.

Now here was Dove, laughing, a full-throated sound of male pleasure, and a tingle spread through her insides. Unable to contain herself, she put down her book. "Something is obviously amusing you."

He looked up. "The kids are talking about what they thought they'd do when they left school and what they might do. I use some basic counseling techniques to get them to understand there is hope in the world. Some of them saw really bad stuff, and it's left them trying to work out what's okay and what isn't. That's hard for eight and nine year olds to work through."

Leonie blinked. "You're really an amazing man."

Dove stilled and looked at her. "I'm just an ordinary person, Leonie."

"Umm, not really. You work with the kids, you counsel people who are dealing with a huge and life-altering event. You give hope. And you garden. The perfect package, some might say."

His face shuttered. "I'm a priest and a man. Nothing more. Nothing less."

She bit her lip. "I'm sorry, Dove. I didn't mean to offend you."

Dove scrubbed a hand over his face as he sighed. "No, it's okay. I don't feel comfortable being placed on a pedestal is all. I'm just a normal person doing what has to be done in unusual times."

Why couldn't he see he did so much more than just what had to be done?

Sliding the book from her lap to the chair beside her, she reached out. "No one is putting you on a pedestal, but they are thankful for you. The man they respect and trust." She touched his knee and felt the strength of him through the denim. The *manliness*.

His gaze captured hers. "I'm a man, Leonie."

Were his words a warning or a promise?

Leonie swallowed, mouth suddenly dry. "I guess I should head to bed."

He nodded in silence, and Leonie rose.

"Good night, Dove." She padded to the door and turned the handle before swinging back. "Don't underestimate yourself." On those words, she retreated.

Chapter 4

Dove tossed and turned, his body betraying an interest in the woman who lay feet from him, in the next room. It wasn't the first time he'd felt interest or even sexual hunger. He was a man, after all. But he was also a priest and entering a casual, sex-driven relationship didn't fit with his beliefs.

He wanted a family. Children. But how could he lead the flock if his own decisions were poorly conceived?

So, he ruthlessly contained himself as he looked out the window into the night. The howls of the dogs beyond the barrier echoed in the silence. Rising in frustration, he moved to the window when a sound from within his home alerted him that Leonie was also having a bad night. Scooping up his dressing gown, he hurried silently to the door and pulled it open.

A whimper sounded, and he ignored all the internal alarms that told him this wasn't the brightest idea and entered her room.

She was asleep, yet silvery tear tracks glistened on her face. The open curtain allowed him full view of the woman tangled in the sheets before him, her nightshirt having ridden up to her belly and only a pair of tiny panties covering her mound.

Dove reached out and carefully pulled the sheet over her then settled onto the side of the bed, touching her shoulder as she whispered, "Gary."

Her brother's name, and he knew what she saw. "Leonie, wake up. It's a nightmare."

She writhed and cried a little more, and Dove shook her harder. "Leonie, wake up."

Leonie started awake, eyes wide, mouth rounded as if she were about to scream. "Dove?" Her voice shook, and she launched herself into his arms, nestling as if this was the only safety she could find. "I saw it all."

Dove folded his arms around her, his fingers tracing soft circles, hoping to comfort, but his body knew the touch of a woman—particularly this one—and responded by hardening.

He squeezed his eyes shut, cursing the weakness of the man as he settled her more comfortably in his arms. "It's okay, Leonie. I'm here, and you're safe now. Here with me."

She shuddered and held on, arms wound around him like vines. "I am safe here, aren't I, Dove? I'm not going to be sent away like the girls from my hometown?"

"I won't let anyone send you away." He wouldn't allow that to happen, because there was something, an emotion growing deep inside him, that would do anything to keep her close.

"Dove?"

"Yes?"

"Will you…" She cleared her throat. "…kiss me please?" Her words were tremulous, and he squeezed his eyes a little tighter together in response, seeking the strength to make the right decision. He just didn't know which one he should make.

"I…" He swallowed because that's what his body wanted. That and so much more, as his groin tightened.

Now Leonie pulled away, disentangling herself, and he opened his eyes with surprise. "I shouldn't have asked that."

In the light of the moon, he could see how red her eyes were, the traces of tears still on her cheeks, and the shimmer of moisture on her lashes. She looked so lost and alone.

His mind snapped. He didn't think, merely leaned forward, and a heartbeat later his lips settled on hers.

He swallowed her squeak of surprise, lost in the softness of her skin. Reaching out, he tugged her gently toward him, so their bodies touched lightly.

Her lips opened, and the sweetness of her breath welcomed his tongue as it surged deep within.

Leonie shook in his embrace, and that woke him from the dream he'd somehow moved into wide awake.

"Leonie, I shouldn't have done that." He felt guilty for having taken advantage of her in this state.

Her face paled further, and hurt flashed in her eyes. "No, it's really my fault," she muttered.

Dove sighed. "No, I don't mean I'm sorry I kissed you. Just the timing. You had a nightmare, and I took advantage."

Her hair whipped back and forth as she shook her head. "No. I asked, remember?" She grasped his hand. "I wanted it. You're a sexy man, and I found comfort in your arms."

"And you're in an unusual situation right now, Leonie. You're grieving and feeling guilty. You're needing a human connection, and I'm here and unattached. It's not unusual. Look, how about I go make us a cup of tea?"

He rose, but before he could leave, her hand gripped his. "Maybe and maybe not. I don't know all the answers, but what I do know is I'm interested, Dove. I find you to be a man I can both respect and trust."

He snorted. "I think a cup of tea is definitely in order, and I'll tell you a story." It was the one he didn't want to share, but she had to know it all. Everything. After that she'd likely change her mind about the respect and trust thing.

He stomped to the kitchen and filled the kettle, aware she'd padded in seconds after him and watched his actions. More than likely she'd be mystified by what he was about to tell her.

Once they'd settled at the table, he inhaled deeply, hands wound around the hot drink, letting the heat dispel the sudden cold that filled him up. "After Leroy and Julia came, they went on a mission.

We had to find a zombie that had been taken by the militia. They roamed around, collecting species for experimentation. They brought a sample back, and Ramon headed the team investigating the virus. Afterward, I told Liam I'd heard of a small lab south of here. I offered to go because Leroy couldn't. He wasn't in any fit state. The PTSD had him really wound up."

In his mind, Dove could see the scenes. The people involved. The decisions he'd made as leader.

"Jamie and I were sent down with a group of six others. We left on bikes early, searching first for some bolt-holes we could add to our lists." Every word he spoke came at a cost. His fingers shook as he explained the situation. "We were gone for about four days when we found the first nest. Small and not well-guarded. There was a female guard on duty, and there were only a couple of militia members. They were in charge of some who hadn't transitioned to the mutations all that well, we think. It was…" Dove stumbled here, then firmed his shoulders. "I decided to watch for a couple of days, hide in a small house nearby, and take turns to see what was going on. On about the seventh day, one of the team came back. He'd heard they were going to truck the zombies out. Release them near one of the smaller compounds to assess their strength and *hunger*. Whether they'd survive given they were 'compromised' already."

Heaven knew just saying the words cost him. But it was what would come next that would forever haunt him.

"We had to stop them, so I sent the team out to neutralize the threat. Because I wasn't able to finish them, I took the female guard prisoner while the others exterminated the zombies. I was to guard her, see what information I could glean. We brought her into the house and tied her up so she couldn't escape and alert anyone else. I was just getting the information we needed when it seems one of the zombies escaped our people. He broke in. I tried to release her, but Jamie arrived as it attacked. He saved me. The guard, who was called Ellen, didn't make it out."

Leonie's mouth settled into an 'o' and she snaked out a hand. "You feel guilty?"

His mirthless laugh couldn't hide his loathing for himself. "Yeah.

If we'd been faster, or the team had been bigger..." He cursed and turned away. When he turned back, he let her see the anguish and regret in his eyes. "I'd argued that a small team was best, so we wouldn't be noticed." The words were bile-coated, bitter, and full of self-recrimination. "She died because I thought I knew best." He turned away, tugging his hand from hers, and not for the first time he tangled it in his hair; the brief instant of pain the only surcease he'd allow himself.

"Who counsels the counselor?" Her words, quiet and understanding, bit deep.

The tears he'd refused to allow to fall escaped now. "Leonie, it's my fault. I'm not a good man."

"Bullshit! You did what you had to. Did you gain information to assist others?" Leonie's voice took on a hard edge. "Did you make a difference?"

He whipped around. "They got a fresh sample, and yes, we saved lives by stopping the release." The knowledge meant nothing could ever absolve him from the decisions he'd made. He'd led the team because it was his plan, based on what he'd heard while in the course of his work with others.

"So, lives were saved. Were there other positives?"

Dove swiped at the moisture on his face. "The female guard told us where the main camp was and other smaller ones. Plans were drawn up, and yes, we closed them down, but there are still mutated zombies out there. They released a couple of batches before—"

"Okay, so you did what you had to. It's a war, Dove. People die."

"But I'm a *priest!*" He shot up from the table, scouring fury urging him on. "I'm not supposed to be involved. I'm not supposed to let others die!"

Now Leonie moved closer. She slid her arms around him and stopped his agitated pacing by placing her head against his chest. "You saved me and probably thousands of others. You give comfort and hope. The situation wasn't meant to go like that, was it? You were going to bring her back here. Attempt to rehabilitate her, I bet. Am I right?"

Dove stilled and thrust his head back to stare at the ceiling. He couldn't answer in the affirmative, although that had indeed been the plan.

"Dove? I'm pretty sucky at the Bible and remembering verses, but I'll bet there's one about asking for forgiveness because God forgives all, right?"

"*He has not punished us as we deserve for all our sins, for his mercy toward those who fear and honor him is as great as the height of the heavens above the earth,*" Dove intoned, remembering the verse well. "Psalm 103," he murmured.

"And?"

"Ahh, you're good." He closed his eyes and inhaled, searching for the balance inside himself. "It's easier said than done though. He might forgive me, but I'm a man, and forgiving myself is a lot harder."

Chapter 5

Leonie dressed slowly, taking care with her hair and tying it back into a ponytail. Today Dove was going to take her to Ramon for her medical, then on to see about work rosters.

Weariness dragged at her. After last night's mutual counseling session she wondered how Dove was coping. He'd been pretty well banged around by the confession of his mission, and she wondered how he managed, living alone.

Leaving the bedroom felt like a major effort, but she found Dove standing in the kitchen, kettle in hand. "Coffee?"

She shook her head. "I think a tea might be better. Do you happen to have any green tea?"

Cocking his head, Dove looked at her. "Not here, but I think there's some in the store. Want me to get you some?" Such a nice, familiar comment, and yet it felt odd to be talking to this man in his kitchen as if they were… *Nuh-uh. Don't go there, Leonie.*

"No, whatever you have will be fine, thanks, Dove." She wandered to the counter. "Can I do anything for you?"

He smiled widely. "Lay the table for me? I've got some cereals and toast. Bread was freshly baked yesterday."

The sight of his grin had her heart thumping a faster than usual beat. "Sure."

She settled to the task, and he carried the drinks, boxes of cereal, and a bottle of milk to the table. She noted a small pat of butter on a plate. "They make their own butter too?"

"Well, we have farmers, cooks, teachers, mechanics, and electricians. A doctor and families. There's a wealth of knowledge, and people put it to good use once they realized we needed to be self-sustaining."

"Oh wow! I don't suppose there's movie nights though. I mean that would be asking—"

"There's DVDs. I think they raided the libraries and stores soon after it all happened. Sometimes they set up a screen, data projector, and sound system in the refectory. Usually when things are tough and the community needs something to raise their spirits."

Leonie blinked. They had cobbled together a community, trying to meet both their physical and emotional needs. "I'm really pleased to be here." She reached out and brushed her hand over his. "And I'm really pleased to have found a friend already."

He inclined his head to the side. "Is that what you want? A friend?" There was a question in his eyes, one she wasn't ready to investigate deeply because…he was a *priest*. It felt wrong. Dirty and furtive.

Instead of telling him those things though, she opted for, "For now, Dove."

His eyes hooded and he nodded. "Then I'll be your friend, Leonie."

The words he didn't say, the ones she needed to hear, were '*until you need more*', yet they were there in his gaze.

DOVE WALKED wide circles around Leonie for three weeks before he felt it was time to broach the subject of her moving into the singles accommodation. Proximity had become an increasing issue for him. She wanted a friend but daily his attachment to her grew.

He'd wake in the morning and make tea and coffee. The table set for two.

In the evenings she was there to talk about his day and hers.

She'd even rearranged a little to make the rooms feel more welcoming. Things he hadn't known they could be until a woman's touch made them happen.

He'd find his washing done and folded, sitting on the bed, or the bathroom shining after she'd cleaned it. Little things that made him feel she cared about him as more than just the priest, but as a man and a person. His heart responded by needing to be around her. That yearning grew daily.

Tonight he'd returned to the house to find her folding his clothing yet again, with dinner cooking. She'd raised her face to him with a bright smile. "Hey, Dove. Dinner's cooking, and I'm just finishing the washing. Go grab a shower, and I'll have a drink ready when you come out."

His hunger for her company, as Leonie and a woman, constantly grew harder—if he could pardon the pun—to keep under wraps. She'd looked adorable in cotton shorts and a tiny top that bared her shoulders. Her skin had taken on a healthy glow in the weeks she'd been with him. The haunted look she'd worn for days had melted away, and the talented and caring woman took over.

He'd showered and changed, accepted the piles of washing and stashed them before joining her at the stool for the iced tea she'd made.

"How was your day?" he began.

"Fabulous. The kids are getting used to being in a classroom, and even though we had to have an incursion drill, they're moving quicker and more as a group."

Liam had insisted the kids should all be drilled in how to react should a zombie attack happen, because he'd told them being alert was an important part of keeping their community healthy.

"That's great. So, you're settled in now?" The question stuck hard in his throat.

"Well, yes. But that leads me to something I wanted to discuss with you." Her voice took on a serious note, and he waited. "I…

Um… Oh, how do I start?" Leonie twisted her hands. "I like you. A lot."

"You want to move out. Into the singles units?" Dove prompted.

Her gaze whipped to his, panic and something else flaring in her eyes.

His gut clenched. "What? You can tell me anything."

"That's just it. I don't want to move out." She spoke quietly, and he absorbed the blow.

"Leonie? What do you want?" A flare of hope rooted in his chest.

"You, Dove." She reached for his hands. "I've come to know you in the last few weeks. I want a family, and so do you."

"Why me?"

Her gaze didn't waver. "Because I think I could love you."

It wasn't quite the answer he'd hoped for, but it was honest. "I don't do casual, Leonie."

She nodded. "I know. I don't either." Biting her lip, she scooted closer. "But even more, I'm coming to realize how I feel about living here. With you." She leaned in, closing the distance between them. "Kiss me, Dove."

The Lord knew he wanted to. But they both deserved more than wishes and hopes. "No. I can't."

She whipped away as if he'd struck her. "But… We could get married and…"

Dove winced. "I'd love to marry you, but you don't love me, and to be honest, that's a deal-breaker. For me, marriage is sacred. Something God grants. You have to understand, I can't just jump into something like that." Reaching out, he cupped her face. "I do want you. I'd marry you in a heartbeat if you loved me. But you don't." He brushed his thumb over her lip. "What you're talking about is stability, loneliness and the need of a survivor to form a relationship. It's understandable, but not enough to build a life on." He rose and left the table, paced back and forth then stopped. "I'm leaving tomorrow to visit some of the outlying camps. Jamie and I will be gone for about a week. I need to pack tonight and plan a route."

She rose, her face pale again. "Dinner?"

"How soon will it be ready?" The sudden emotional distance between them felt like a dagger in his gut, but he had to break the dependency they clearly both felt.

"About now?" she whispered.

Guilt coursed, because on her face he read sadness and hurt. He wanted to call back his words, but it wouldn't be fair. Or right.

They ate in silence, then he excused himself.

LEONIE STEWED. "He's going away, and he doesn't think what I feel is real."

She could understand his concerns. Hell, she'd had more than a few of her own as her emotions had risen to the surface.

Yes, she felt guilt at surviving when Gary and the others hadn't. She really did question at first if the emotions she'd felt were about him. But in the weeks she'd been there, she'd been asked to attend everything from a garden planting to a house-raising party. One of the other teachers, a single guy, Joe, had asked her out more than once. While she'd liked him well enough, it wasn't the same kind of *liking* she had for Dove. With him it was more a 'I can't wait 'til he's home to tell him what I've been doing', or even a 'he's so fabulous and makes me feel welcome and special'. All little things, but that didn't even take into account the way her body reacted around him. *Now there's another whole story!*

Now he was going to be away for a week. Heading into zombie-infested areas to undertake his role as priest. It made her feel downright nervous. What if something happened to him? It wasn't the kind of loss she'd felt with her parents, sister, or brother though. This was more a 'how can life go on without the good man sitting here beside me' kind of thoughts.

All this didn't solve her dilemma though: how to show Dove that what she felt was more than a passing phase or part of the healing process.

When he finally opened his bedroom door, she was waiting for him. He looked startled and more than a little weary, and for a moment, she wavered. "Dove, do you have a couple of moments to talk?"

When he nodded there was a hesitancy about him. He settled on the lounge chair, and she slid down beside him, caught his hand in hers. "Okay, so here's the thing. What I'm feeling isn't survivor's guilt, but I know you're uncomfortable. I understand your concern, so when you return, I'm going to move into the singles unit. Give you some space."

He shook his head. "No."

She opened her mouth to argue and he turned. "The units are full."

"Oh. Okay then. So, I'll stay here but out of your way until you're as sure as I am. Secondly, I'm going to join a few groups. There's one starting that's a gardening group. They're going to teach propagation, and I could use that with the kids. Plus, you don't have a real house garden and would benefit from one."

She cleared her throat when he raised an eyebrow.

"Here's my one request. You be careful and stay safe while I'm away. I know I don't have any claim on you, but I'll worry about you while I'm gone. Use that time to think about me. To consider what I'm saying, because while I understand your concern, it's not based on anything except your fear, Dove. I'll be here, waiting for you at the camp."

Leonie rose to leave then muttered a quiet expletive and sank back down, leaning forward to kiss him.

The heat scorched her as their lips moved in time, hands reaching and gripping tight. Her body was a mass of hunger for this man, and it throbbed and hummed as she moaned into the embrace.

Pulling away took every ounce of willpower she had, and she saw he was just as affected as her. "Remember that while you're away, Dove."

Now she rose and left him.

In the bedroom she sighed and slumped onto the bed, reaching for the tiny journal she'd begun since arriving. It allowed her to work through her emotions because they'd been such a jumbled mess. In the past few weeks it was the references to Dove that she noted more and more.

This wasn't some girlish crush though. She'd had them like most girls.

The pen was a small silver one she'd found in the stores. She'd always kept one in her journal for ease of having something to hand. Today, she felt she needed that reassurance of continuity as she opened the journal.

Wednesday 5th

Where do I even begin? Tonight, I tried to explain how I felt to Dove, but it's difficult. He's trying so hard to support me in my grief that he won't acknowledge that what I feel might really be true. He's also ignoring his feelings. I don't know why. It could be he feels responsible for me. That I don't need.

Now he's leaving tomorrow. I'm terrified something will happen to him, and my first thought is to ask him to stay. To just be safe with me behind these gates. I know that's unfair, and that's why I haven't done it. Besides, as I said to him tonight, neither of us has any claim on the other, but I'm trying hard. What I don't get is his need to go.

I feel like I'm tearing myself inside out. I must be supportive of him, but it's not easy, especially when I know what I want. I want him. As my husband, lover, and best friend.

How do I tell him that and make him know I mean it? How do I make him understand that though I feel grief, this is apart from that?

I guess I have a week to think it through and to plan.

L

She closed the book and slid it into the bedside chest of drawers and rolled over. The bed was narrow and squeaky, but the shaft of moonlight coming through the window was reassuring and she embraced it, aware it was the same moon he'd see every night they were apart. It wasn't nearly enough, but it was all she could take for granted.

DOVE WOKE EARLY. He wanted to leave before Leonie rose, but that was cowardly. On the other hand, he didn't want to leave her. Her presence soothed the ragged edges he'd barely been aware of until she was there to soothe them.

In so many ways she complemented him. He sighed. "And no more of those kinds of thoughts, Dove."

He gathered up the canvas backpack and threw in some spare clothes. They'd be traveling by motorbike and light was the only way to go. This time Jamie had found larger bikes and some saddlebags, and Dove carefully lifted the necessary items for services into them. He'd had a special case crafted, and the larger tote for his religious items and everything was fitted in safely. Though the bag was weighty, he hefted it and its mate over his shoulder and left his room.

Leonie stood in the kitchen, her face pale, and she handed him a package. "Some food for on the road and a flask with clean water."

"Thank you." He spoke quietly and he watched as she bit her now trembling lip.

Unable to help himself, he dipped in and took her lips in a gentle kiss. "I'll be back in a few days."

She nodded her head. "Make sure you are."

Her hand reached out, as if to touch him. He stilled, not sure he'd be able to leave if she touched him again, his body screaming he should stay while his psyche told his feet to move.

The pregnant moment passed, and with no more to say, he swung on the ball of his foot, and the leather boots squeaking on the wood floor, he left the house.

Every step away from Leonie felt like he was tearing himself apart. He kept going, aware that no matter what he wanted, there was no alternative. He was the only man of the cloth in this area. He had responsibilities to his flock.

At the gate, he met Jamie. Two large and squat bikes were waiting for them. Dove fastened the leather saddlebags on and climbed astride one machine as Liam came out of the house he and

Elaine shared with their daughter. "Before you go, there's been mutated zombies noted in the region of some of your stops. They're on the move. Here's a map, make notes where and if you see them. Take all necessary care. If others in the encampments or you need help, Jamie's been equipped with a handheld device and we'll monitor the signal twenty-four-seven. We can send in a squad to retrieve you if necessary, but don't take chances."

Both Dove and Jamie nodded, well aware of what this meant. If the mutated zombies had moved that far, then more would make their way here. "Do you need samples?" Maybe Ramon could tell them if these were next generation, born from the bite of the mutated creatures.

Liam cocked his head. "Only if you can collect them safely."

They both grunted their understanding, and Liam stepped back. With a quick move they started the bikes, the gates opening, and they rode out onto the deserted road.

Hours passed and they came across the first settlement, following the path they'd used before. The settlement was small but growing. They'd reinforced their walls, and once Dove and Jamie entered they were warmly welcomed.

"You've been busy," Dove noted, and the oldest man shook his head.

"We've had some incursions lately. Trying to get to the kids. Can't have that, so we worked night and day to increase our fortifications. Good thing 'cause a couple of big buggers came this way last week. Tried to get in, but we held them off. They got away, but not before we hurt them bad. Haven't seen them since but heard others in the distance."

Dove set up and went about his business. The service was joyful, and the flock stayed back to talk with him. After packing up, he carefully considered everything he'd been told before bunking down for the night in the traveler's room they set aside for his and Jamie's use. And in the morning, come sunrise, they were back on their bikes again.

THE HOUSE HAD ASSUMED a lonely air with Dove gone. Leonie filled the days with class preparation, met with some of the parents and explained some of the things they could do to assist their children who were still struggling with the basics, and headed for the community garden. She'd been assigned a bed of her own, and she weeded it by hand, pleased to have something physical to keep her mind occupied and to tire her body so she slept soundly at night.

After the midday meal on the third day, Elaine came out and hunkered down beside her, the baby slung from her chest in a sling. "How are you settling in? Liam says you're still at Dove's because we've run out of accommodation units."

"His place is great. It almost feels like being back to normal, if you know what I mean?"

Elaine smiled. "We've tried really hard to make it as comfortable as we can, but the continued growth is pushing our limits a little. When we set up the original settlement, we had no idea we'd have so many people here. We now have nearly five hundred living in the community full time. But anyway, how are you finding Dove?"

Leonie bit her lip. "He's great." She'd need to be cautious, because if she didn't know better, she'd say Elaine had been sent to scout out if she and Dove were an item.

"Good, that's great." Elaine's response was strange, as if there were another underlying message. "One of the singles units has become available. Since you're next on my list, I'm letting you know you can move in today. I've got the team preparing it as we speak."

The news wasn't what Leonie hoped to hear, but Elaine was smiling as if she'd somehow pulled off the deal of the century.

How should she respond? After all, she'd told Dove she'd be waiting.

"Now, I told Dove when he enquired, that as soon as one was available, I'd make sure you were next on the list, given he's really a private soul."

The words were a blow to the gut. "He asked?"

Elaine nodded. "A couple of days before he left. Said he understood you needed your own space so you could come to terms with what had happened to you. So, it's all done. You are happy about that, aren't you?" Elaine peered at her, and it took every ounce of willpower to stop the shock Leonie felt from appearing on her face.

"Yeah. Sure." Leonie stood up, brushing her hands against the sides of her pants. "Well, I guess I better go collect my stuff from Dove's. Umm, where do I go?" The words were said with forced gaiety as the lump in her stomach congealed.

"Oh, I'll have Maura show you. It's the off-site resort block, but there's a team of guards on hand. Anyway, Maura will be at my house soon. Go grab your stuff and she'll meet you there. If you need more boxes, see the store, and they'll give you one for the relocation."

"Okay. Thanks." Leonie made a hasty retreat, but as she scurried to Dove's the heat of embarrassment scorched her. *He doesn't want you there. Get over it.*

She let herself into the tiny shed house and looked around. Every corner in her mind echoing with his presence. The spot where they'd first kissed. Where he'd helped her to prepare a meal.

"You talked yourself into this corner, Leonie. Time to get yourself out of it." Because surely, this was his way of saying he didn't want what she was offering. Her chest caught as tears rolled down her cheeks.

She scrubbed them away furiously and marched to the bedroom. The small boxes she'd used to transport her stuff sat on the floor beside the chest of drawers, and she lifted them to the bed. Every piece of clothing she neatly folded and slid into them, ensuring her journal and pen were included. In the bathroom, she removed all her toiletries and stashed them in a bag. The books she had borrowed went into another box, and as she looked around, for the first time, she saw that nothing else of herself filled the space.

Hefting the pile of boxes, she tromped out the door, carefully closing it behind her. She'd grab new linens from the store for the beginning of the next phase of her life, she told herself, and she turned for Elaine and Liam's house. Outside stood a mature-aged lady, flanked by three men, each armed with either a rifle or a sword.

"Leonie?" The woman carried a smaller box with her, and when

Leonie nodded, she handed it over. "We've already sent the basics ahead. Kitchen equipment, food, and linens. These are keys and a few other welcome items. We should get going, as the woman who was in the unit has already vacated it. She's moving to another camp so there's no issues there."

Leonie fell into step with the woman and men moving briskly. Juggling the boxes was difficult, and one of the men grabbed two off her. "Let me help you."

He smiled, and she was thankful for the assistance but didn't want to encourage any interest. Not yet. Now she just wanted silence and privacy to lick her wounds. Tears burned, but she blinked them back. *Not now. Not here.*

"Thanks," she said.

They left the secure zone, the well-reinforced gate clanging shut behind them. Now the men's eyes turned hard. They scanned from side to side, and she felt exposed. Nerves thrummed as they moved at a rapid pace. Up one abandoned street, down another, and past houses, silent and shabby with untended gardens, until they reached another fence. This one was not so well-erected, the concrete bases scarred and the mesh sagging.

Her stomach dropped.

"Don't be taken in by the fencing. The reinforcements inside are what matters," the man who held her boxes said.

They pushed open the gate, and she heard the groan of metal, then they moved inside the perimeter. Once the gate was locked they trooped up to the doors, and she could see the lower façade of the building was actually metal. They banged on the door, and it echoed loudly before opening. The door resembled one on a bank vault, and she wondered, not for the first time, how they'd cope in a fire or some similar kind of event.

The door shuttered behind them as they headed up the gloomy corridor to the stairs. "There's three storeys in this building and the same in the other two buildings behind. It used to be a resort, so there's a pool, large refectory area, and gym," Maura explained. "You're on the third floor. Two bedrooms, so lots of room, and a small kitchenette."

"Oh, great." Leonie tried hard to infuse positivity into her words, but it didn't sound honest to her hearing.

"We thought you'd need an office, for planning or whatever teachers do, so the bed and furniture will be removed from the second bedroom, and we've got a desk and filing cabinet coming up later today. If you need anything else, let Stuart, the building supervisor, know. He can set up a requisition order for the furnishings if they don't have them in the storage room here."

They stopped at the top of the stairs, and Maura indicated to the door with 303 on it.

"This is yours. I'll leave you to settle in. If you wish to dine in the refectory, the nightly meal is at 1700 hours. Five o'clock," she added as if thinking Leonie couldn't work out military time. "There's a clock on the wall to keep track of time. You'll find a map in the box with the keys so you can find your way there."

The male guard waited for her to open the door and followed her in with the boxes of items. "I live here too. Unit 201. Lucas is my name, and if you'd like to ask anything, I'm happy to help." His face carried a hopeful grin, and she contained the urge to disabuse him of the notion that she was willing or even looking for a man at this time.

"Uh, thanks. I'll probably see you around," Leonie mumbled and slid her boxes on the counter top. "Thanks for this."

He cleared his throat, placing the boxes he carried on the floor. "Guards assemble on the hour from six in the morning to seven at night, both ways. If you need to go to the main compound just wait in the hall downstairs and you'll be escorted over."

She nodded and waited as he headed for the door.

"Maybe I'll see you in the refectory tonight?" Again, that hopeful sound in his voice twisted her guts.

"Maybe," Leonie answered and closed the door behind him.

The lounge was bright. Welcoming but empty. Not at all like Dove's place. Walking to the main bedroom, she peered inside. A pale bedspread, clearly new, and well-plumped pillows, and at the end, three pale green towels, face washers, hand towels, and a spare set of sheets sat in a pile tied with a ribbon.

A balcony was accessed through a sliding glass door, and she stepped out, sighing when she noted a little outdoor setting and a small garden of vegetables and flowers surrounding the table and chairs. "Obviously they liked gardening," Leonie muttered to herself. At least the place wouldn't be stark.

Leaving the door open, she wandered back inside to the lounge, which also had a similar slider, and opened it, so the air whooshed in, freshening the unit.

In the office space she noted the office chair, old-fashioned wood desk, and bookcase. The filing cabinet was topped with notepads and pens. They'd managed to fill the room faster than expected. They'd thought of her needs, and the knowledge of this moved her as she realized she wouldn't need to ask for anything else. "And since everything has already been delivered, I won't have to talk to anyone else today."

It was… She searched her mind, trying to work out what was wrong with this setup. The thing was, the apartment felt soulless without Dove to share this space with her.

"Don't be stupid," she castigated herself, feeling the prick of angry tears forming.

She might have wanted to dwell, but there was work to do. Opening the cupboards and fridge, she took stock of what there was on hand. Basics of flour, some herbs, meat, and eggs. Vegetables.

The seasonality of the offerings wasn't lost on her, and for the first time, she yearned for some of her cookbooks, left behind in the town of her birth. Gathering up the boxes with her things, she started to unpack, now that this was her home.

DOVE PULLED his bike to a stop nearby the remains of the old people mover. Inside he saw the corpses. The birds which had been picking at the bones took to flight with a scream as they had roared up the road on the bikes.

Now Jamie was alert, rifle in his hands. "Sure you want to do this, Dove?"

His senses on high alert, Dove nodded. "We're so close, Jamie. Having some of her photos and possessions will help her to feel more settled, and to be honest, most of us would love to have the things most important to them in these days."

Jamie simply grunted.

Climbing off the bike, Dove advanced, eyes scanning around. This wasn't the place to be taken by surprise. Nearing the vehicle, he noticed the windows had been broken, the rear door wrenched from its hinges.

Bags and a suitcase still sat in the boot. Carefully, he retrieved them. The suitcase was too large to carry, but Jamie's saddlebags were almost empty, so he dragged the items over and opened the suitcase. On the top sat a bridal gown, and he gaped at it. He pushed it aside and noted a tiny box with rings within. Those he stashed in his pocket. Further down he saw a pouch containing photos and scooped it up. "These go in," he muttered.

Some clothes he stashed deep. The rest of the items were a mix of men's clothes, odd toys, and some books, and he added what fit as best he could, filling the first then second saddlebag. He could and should leave the gown behind, but instinct told him this was important to her, so he rolled it carefully and slid it into his own bag where he'd stashed the food Leonie had thrust at him.

With a sigh he retreated, opened the special wooden box he'd drawn out of his saddlebag, and took out the *aspergillum* and holy water. His hands moved instinctively, dipping and spraying the blessed water as he prayed for the souls of those within the vehicle. Before they left, Jamie would light it up, so their bodies would not be further violated.

"Go forth good Christian souls on your journey from this world…" Whether they shared his faith or not, he would do all he could to commend their souls to peace in the hereafter.

With the rite completed, he placed the items back into their box, stashed it in the saddlebag, and nodded to Jamie. The large man took the bottles of flammable liquids, removed the caps, and stuffed a wad of fabric inside before continuing to wind it around the bottles. Then he lit them and threw them into the remains, and they started their bikes.

A *whoosh* sounded behind them, but they rode on, not looking back. Because that way only ever led to regrets, Dove knew.

It wasn't long until they reached the safe house where Leonie had changed into his clothes. Movement caught his eye as a large, lumbering zombie emerged from within, his eyes red and bulbous.

It shuffled toward them, and three others emerged from the depths as he and Jamie gave the bikes more gas and screamed past swiping hands. They'd fed recently, and his stomach clenched. One nearly caught him with greedy fingers, and his blood thrummed in his veins at the near miss as they roared away.

They rode quickly for several kilometers before Jamie indicated they should stop. Eucalypts edged the old road, the bush starting to encroach on what had previously been open roadway. Soon, it would reclaim where many had traveled before in vehicles.

Once the bikes were silent, they removed their helmets. "Those were big buggers, Dove. Fast and muscled."

Jamie's words reinforced what he'd also noted. *Were they mutated?* They appeared in better condition than some of their decaying counterparts. Bodies appeared intact, and those eyes... Dove shuddered at the memory.

"They don't look like the ones we've seen for some time," Dove said. "They appear to be still in their prime. Makes me think..."

Jamie nodded. "We need to let Liam know, but also the camps nearby. Ensure they're on their guard."

Dove agreed. "But we should be swift. We aren't all that far from home, and they're moving faster than those we're used to."

Not all camps welcomed strangers, and especially those with religion and roaring around on motorbikes. For some, the 'brave new world' they embraced meant returning to old ways. Some of those old ways meant women and children were little more than chattels to use, abuse, and give away to increase their status among their peers. But they'd warn them all the same, because everyone needed to be aware of these creatures in their vicinity. So once more they started the bikes and roared off along the road.

Chapter 6

Leonie trudged across the road, part of the small knot of people returning home after a day of work; some in the field, some in the kitchens, and at least one young woman in the hospital. In the last few days, Leonie had caught her name and sidled up to Beth. The woman was little more than a girl and explained she'd been in her first year of high school when the world had changed. Now she was a nurse, working with Ramon. Leonie liked her and saw a kindred spirit. Her eyes were dark with a sadness that found its twin in Leonie's breast. She'd lost everyone who was important to her. First her parents and sister, then Gary. Those losses tore at her, but it was Dove that struck deep. As if part of herself had been removed.

On a deep breath, Leonie took a chance. "Beth, would you like to join me for dinner?"

The girl looked up, startled. "I um… Sure."

"Great. I'm in 303."

"Okay, what time, Leonie?"

"Anytime that suits. We'll sit on the balcony and watch the sun go down."

They entered the building, hearing the clang of the door shuttering. Before they could leave, Stuart, the old supervisor of the building, waved his hand, gaining their attention. In his sixties with grizzled gray hair and his face deeply lined, he barely spoke a word unless it was important. The guards were always full of chatter and shared that Stuart's stutter had affected his confidence but not his ability to look after the building.

"As...as you kn...know there has been talk of mut...mutated zombies. We've heard they're in th...the region. All guards to and fr...from will be doubled."

The room erupted as concerns flew and questions too. Stuart raised his hands. "We do...don't have much more infor...mation." Now he turned and moved up the stairs, ending the assembly, and they milled around for a moment before heading for their individual units.

Leonie made her way up the steps, wondering if Dove and Jamie had returned yet. It had been six days since they'd left. Would he come looking for her or breathe a sigh of relief that she'd left his home?

Her guts twisted as she stepped up to her door, unlocking it and entering the unit. "Don't be stupid, Leonie. You've got work to mark, tomorrow's lessons to plan, and Beth is joining you for dinner. Stop dwelling on him and get on with your life." *If only it were that simple.*

Leonie focused on the tasks she'd set herself. She watered the plants and breathed in the clear air.

In her office, she deposited the sheets and booklets her students used and set to work, looking at what they'd achieved and considering how to improve on their outcomes. In a small notepad, she wrote down her plan for the next day. Considering the age of her students, and their experience of books and reading, it was hard work, as most had little formal education before starting in her class.

Dinner was cooking in the kitchen, a stew of chicken and seasonal veggies, and not for the first time, she yearned for strawberries and melons—her favorite fruits. But at least they had nutritious and filling foods. More than she'd experienced in such a long time.

"I just need to accept that my life is full of disappointments and make the best of it."

On the table, Leonie spied her journal and scooped it up.

Tuesday 11th
Today we were told that there could be mutated zombies in the area. I
have to admit, I'm afraid. I know we live in a reinforced building, but
if what some of the others have said is correct, then they're stronger and
faster? Capable of thinking for themselves? That makes me nervous.
What if they can get past the metal sheeting? Are we safe? I guess we
will have to wait and see.
I wonder if Dove has returned. He's been gone for a week, which is how
long he said he'd be away. I haven't seen him, and I wonder if that
means something.
Ha! Knowing me, I'm overthinking it.
Maybe he's not back yet, or busy. I just don't know what to think or
how to react right now. It feels like my life is out of my control, and I
don't like that much. I guess I'll have to be patient though.
Beth is joining me for dinner tonight. She seems nice. Young but willing
to make the best of what we have, though I think in her life there's been
something dark. She always seems sad. Maybe we can support each
other?
The kids are making progress. Some faster than others, but like everyone
else they've seen things that are hard to forget. Every day we have a
session now, where we talk about the good things. They need positives to
hold onto, otherwise why the hell are we even bothering?

Reading over the words, Leonie noted the negativity. "Come on.
Find a positive. Something good to end this on." She looked over at
the small balcony and saw a flower bud, the first of the season,
reaching up to the light.

Today, my garden on the balcony had the first bud show itself. Soon
there'll be a flower. I wonder what kind it is and the color. It reminds
me that there is always hope. That's why we continue.
L

With a snap, Leonie closed the journal and nodded. Yes, the

right way to end it. On something good. Rising, she headed for the bathroom before returning to the balcony. A knocking at the door told her Beth had come to join her.

She called, "Come on in, Beth." She glanced back down to the flowers and debated watering them.

"It's not Beth." Dove's voice had her whirling. "You left," he said, the unhappiness in his words a jolt.

"You asked Elaine to find me somewhere. She did." Leonie stepped into the room and he joined her, closing the door behind him. The scent of him filled her senses. "I'll make you a—" Before she could finish the words, he'd caught her to him, hard against his chest, and was kissing her. Little flickers of physical fireworks sparking in her veins.

Her mind whirled, and when Dove released her, all she could do was stare at the unshaven man before her.

"I didn't know where you were until Elaine told me," he said. "Come back. Come home."

Those words thrilled her. "But..."

"No buts. Come back with me, Leonie. Please."

Her gut clenched. "You don't do casual relationships." The words hung between them in the air, but she had to know. Needed him to tell her exactly what he wanted.

"I know. Marry me."

Her eyes widened as shock slammed into her. *Marriage.* She really hadn't expected that. She knew she felt deeply about him, thought it could be love, but this?

"Leonie? Say something. Say yes." His words drugged her. Yearning began blooming like a flower in her chest.

"I... *Why?*"

"I don't want to be without you. What I feel for you, it's not just sexual need. We get along well. You're alone, and so am I. We both feel guilty but want to make a difference. We can do that together. And the hunger between us? It's big and consuming. Say yes." His fingers gripped hers, holding her close. Urging her to make a decision.

She wanted to say yes. She wanted everything he offered. But she wanted more too. She wanted love.

"I… If I say yes, what if it goes wrong? What if you decide you don't want me?"

"Leonie, I can't tell you what lies ahead. I can't peer into the future and give you guarantees. But I can give you this. Me."

Biting her lip, she turned away.

She heard him move behind her. "I found the gown and your photos, and I found these too." Dove stepped in front of her, his hand unfurling and showing her the wedding rings and engagement ring both her parents had worn right up until their deaths. She vividly remembered the day the hospital nurse had placed them in her hand after their passing.

There was so much history associated with them, and yet even more important was what he'd done. For her. "You went back."

"The photos were important to you. They were still there, Leonie. I did what I could for your brother and those in the car. I hope they'll rest in peace now." Dove's words set her eyes tearing up.

"I… Thank you." Those rings and the promise in them undid her, and in that second, the decision was made. "Yes. I will."

His hand reached out and cupped her cheek, not that she could see for the fall of liquid that filled her gaze. "I will do everything I can to make you happy. I will always be honest and true. On that you have my word."

She closed her eyes as his lips found hers. The gentleness nearly undoing her. It was a glance and a wish, then she opened her eyes to find him watching her. "What now, Dove?"

"We go home."

Those words filled her with joy. Could it really be that simple? "I have things I need."

He nodded. "I'll help you. Show me what you need immediately."

She pointed him to the office. "The papers, books, and stuff. I'll grab my clothes and toiletries."

Speed felt like it was necessary, and she moved into the

bedroom. Leonie had only just filled the first box and started loading up her clothes when she heard banging and thudding.

"What…" She hurried into the lounge to see that Dove had beaten her there. He wrenched open the door. The cacophony on the level below him was wild.

He paled and shoved her back. "Go in. Stay inside until I come for you. Stay away from the windows."

He thrust the door shut and she was once again alone.

THE INSTANT DOVE heard the first roars, he knew what was happening. It revived memories of trying to shield the girls in the sacristy. The day the school had been attacked, leaving him the only survivor.

His gut churned. No way would he allow Leonie to become another statistic in this mess. He'd do whatever he could to protect her.

Looking over the railing of the concrete stairs, he glanced down. The men wrestled with an enormous creature. Gunfire sounded, alerting the broader community to the incursion. All that was needed was for the guards to hold their ground for moments, then help would come. Already he heard in the distance the toll of the bell, which they'd erected at every gate to alert to danger.

The monster pushed closer to where a man held a large shield. The zombie caught sight of Dove and roared. Its red eyes seemed to pulse, and Dove knew he had to do something. He carefully made his way down the stairs, lips moving silently in a prayer of absolution and a request for help as he moved closer to the guards. He could see one was injured, scarlet blood already seeping through the cloth of his clothes. He'd need medical assistance.

Dove reached the bottom of the stairs as help arrived. The large attacker whirled, but the guards were ready; nets of light metal swung and covered the creature while someone called, "Tranq, get out of the way!"

The *pszzt* of the pressure gun they'd modified echoed, and

though the zombie fought hard, with arms flying, mouth wide open to display red and black teeth, he slowed. Then stilled.

When he toppled it was hard, crashing down on the injured man, and Dove swung into action.

"Let me take a look at that." He tore the man's shirt, trying to get to the wound. The marks he saw made his blood run cold. Bitten.

"I don't wanna die. I wanna live. Please!"

Dove's gut clenched. "You need to see Ramon straight away." He turned and saw Liam and Ramon fighting their way forward through the throng assembled. "He's going to need emergency care. Bite mark."

Ramon scowled. "Damn it. We'll get him out of here and into a holding location."

The holding locations were little more than cells made of concrete and reinforced steel. It was all they had to hold them until they could assess how the body would react to the bite. So far, the fatality rate was one hundred percent.

Liam looked at Dove. "You found her?" He was, of course, talking about Leonie, and Dove gave a very short nod. "Good. We need to talk. Tonight. I can come to you?"

"Yeah. Look, bring Elaine with you. I need you to attend in an official capacity anyway. Bring the camera." He turned and headed for the stairs, noting the men had already hoisted the injured man up and were carrying him away as he appeared to fall into unconsciousness. "Give me a couple of hours, so around seven?"

He felt the burn of Liam's gaze but ignored it. Right now, he needed to check Leonie and get her back to the house, where she'd be safe. He guessed Liam would arrange alternative housing for the rest of the building's inhabitants until after repairs and further fortifications could be put in place. It wouldn't be safe right now.

At Leonie's door, he stopped and inhaled deeply, aware of the gravity of the agreement they were about to make to each other. When he knocked and called her name, she flung open the door and wound her arms around his neck. "I was worried, Dove. Are you okay?" Leonie's voice was muffled by the shirt, having put her face against his chest, like she was trying to squirrel inside his body.

"I'm fine. But I want you home. Now. Safe." For a moment he hugged her tight, then released her. "Let's get your things."

She moved away, and he felt the loss of her heat. "I've got a lot." Her face turned red, and he grinned.

"So, we make two trips."

Leonie shook her head, hair flying around her face. "Nuh-uh. Once we're gone, that's it. I don't feel safe here and…" She licked her lips. "I'm just feeling on edge, okay?"

"Then we'd better find a way to juggle all this stuff." He slid around her, checking the kitchen cupboard, and blinked. "What do you plan—"

"There's a girl downstairs. I'll give her the key and she can come help herself and share it around if she wants." Her hand flew to her mouth. "Dinner!" Into the kitchen she went, moving a pot from the stove and lifting the lid. "Caught it just in time. I'll leave it for the guys downstairs. It's stew." She glanced at Dove. "Unless you want me to bring it home?"

Shaking his head, he beckoned her back with an extended hand. "No. We'll arrange something better. After all, tonight is a celebration."

He noted the way she gulped.

"But only if you're ready and sure?" he added.

"I am," Leonie answered, and the bubble of anxiety inside his chest disappeared.

"Good."

Now they gathered the boxes and the files. They had to juggle but managed it all in a single, though fraught, trip. The guards had been tripled, with Liam remaining behind until he was sure everyone was moved to a new and secure location.

Dove felt better once they'd moved inside the gates, but doubted that even here they'd be safe. Knowing what he did now, having seen the mutates with his own eyes, the knowledge lodged itself in his brain. He'd have to discuss all this with Liam and the rest of the board at their next meeting.

Opening the door to his house, Dove stepped inside his—*their,* his brain corrected—home. When Leonie stepped in the direction of her bedroom, he cleared his throat and she turned then an 'o' formed on her mouth.

"Our bedroom." He indicated to the door, and she nodded. Together they carried her clothes and toiletries, and he marveled at how right it felt.

He made room in the drawers and cupboard and pride filled him. His woman. Soon to be his wife.

Then he took her across the lounge to where she'd previously slept in her old bedroom. On the bed, he'd piled the photos and clothes, and laid the wedding gown carefully beside them.

Her face crumpled as she reached for it. The old-fashioned, slightly yellowed material obviously meant a lot to her. "My mother's gown," she whispered, and he understood the importance it held for her.

"You'll wear it?"

Leonie blinked. "For our wedding? But where and how?"

He slipped his hands over her shoulders, keeping a small distance between them but ensuring she knew to listen. "Elaine and Liam will be here later. They'll hear our vows. We can pray together if you like. They're bringing a camera too. To take a photo for us. I'm going to arrange a meal from the refectory so neither of us has to cook. It will be a celebration, intimate but meaningful."

"My hair," she whispered, and he couldn't contain his smile at the feminine complaint.

"You're beautiful, Leonie, just as you are."

Now a tiny frown creased her forehead.

"It's not what you imagined?"

As Leonie shook her head, her hair whipped him. "Not really, no."

"I understand. Do you want more time?" He hated uttering those words, but if that's what she needed, he'd give it to her.

"No. I just need to get ready, I think. Maybe shower and…" Moving away, Leonie reached for the gown on the bed. "I'm going to wear my mother's gown."

Dove reached into his pocket and drew out the three rings. The tiny diamond glinted in the waning light of day. "Will you wear this?"

Leonie extended her hand, and with a trembling hand he slid the ring onto her finger, which fit perfectly, then bent down and kissed it.

"This is my promise to you, Leonie."

Emotion welled. He wanted her, now. Badly. His body ached, so he retreated beyond the door, but before he closed it, he glanced at the clock.

"Two hours, Leonie." The door clicked shut with a tiny snick and he inhaled, his chest tight, before he walked away.

Chapter 7

When the door of the bedroom opened after a knock, Leonie turned in surprise. Elaine entered, her hair tied back in a ponytail. "Dove told us you're getting married!"

Leonie smiled, though she was sure it wobbled a little. "Yes. But my hair's a mess, I've got no makeup, and I don't think I can do the gown up by myself." *God, I sound so vain.*

"No worries. I've brought some reinforcements. Dove likes to do everything small, but he's given a lot to the compound. We thought we'd surprise him a little. Julia is organizing a meal as I speak, and I've brought makeup, and Sarah used to be a hairdresser." Another woman entered the room, a large bag in her arms. "She's going to tizzy your hair. I'll do your makeup, then we can help you into your dress. But before you do, I sent down to the store for some special underwear." Elaine held out a small bag. Leonie took it and peered within. "Pick what you like that suits you."

Shock overcame Leonie, and she looked at the woman before her. "But I…"

"Time's getting short. Dove told me you're down to about an hour and a half."

The other woman—Sarah, she guessed—nodded as if agreeing that time was short.

"Besides, while Sarah's doing her thing, I'm going to feed the baby and get her settled."

Julia entered the room and slid the tiny baby into Elaine's arms, and the bond between mother and baby was instantly obvious.

Elaine moved to the end of the bed and settled down on it, lifting her shirt to offer her breast to the child in her arms.

The woman, Sarah, spoke quietly, "I'm going to set up in the lounge. It's larger." She disappeared back through the doorway.

A sudden sense of right filled Leonie. These women were there to help her celebrate her wedding, and she'd embrace it. "Okay, so what first?" Excitement started to fizz in her veins, and she jittered as she waited for them to set to work.

"Underwear first," suggested Julia, who promptly left the room.

"Come on out when you're ready and we'll begin," Sarah's voice echoed through the doorway.

Leonie headed for the bathroom, changed into the underwear, and tugged on a light robe before she settled on the chair set up and let the woman brush and trim her hair, relaxing at the gentle touches and efficient moves. She felt the fussing, and must have drifted off, because the next thing she knew the woman was chortling, "I think she's dozed off."

"Dove told us about the attack. She's probably exhausted from the fright," Julia added.

Leonie yawned loudly.

"No, she's awake now." Chortles filled the air. "I used to do that when the hairdresser would do my hair. Relaxation-plus if you ask me. Now, Sarah, some wax or just tweeze?" Elaine stood in front of her when Leonie opened her eyes.

"Tweezers only, sorry. But we'll make short work of those brows."

Elaine moved, and Sarah took her place and squatted down.

"Just close your eyes lightly, and we'll tame those brows."

Leonie couldn't help herself; her eyes opened wide. "What… What's wrong with my brows?"

Sarah grinned. "They just need a little shaping, then we'll let Elaine at you with the makeup. We've only got about half an hour, and we've got to get you finished and out front before Dove gets back."

They worked their magic, and finally, dressed in the gown, her feet bare because she'd refused to wear any borrowed shoes for the event, she was ready. Elaine steered her before the mirror, and Leonie gasped. "That's not me."

The woman standing there was beautiful. Hair artfully arranged in careful tendrils that cascaded down her back, lips of ruby, and her eyes wide and shaded to perfection. The gown hugged her body, and the glint of the diamond on her finger twinkled in the lamplight.

"Come on," urged Julia and Elaine together, Sarah having retrieved the baby and left.

They flanked her as she moved to the front door. It opened, and her breath caught. Ribbons led from the door to a makeshift altar under the stars, and there, waiting for her, was Dove.

She stepped forward, and those gathered sighed.

One step, then another brought her to the man she was about to pledge herself to.

He took her hand. Smiled. "You look beautiful," he murmured, leaning in close so only she could hear. He cleared his throat, leaned away, and spoke louder for all to hear. "Leonie, the woman I will wed tonight before God and those gathered here, I make my promises to you. To be faithful, honest, and to care for you for all the days we have together."

She blinked, considered, and answered, "Dove, the man I wed tonight, I will be faithful and honest. I will care for you and any children who come from us. I will honor you and love you, help you, and remain with you in this world and into the next."

His shock was a palpable thing, then he smiled. It gathered in his eyes, leaving them glinting.

He took the rings from his pocket. "May the Lord bless these rings as symbols of our promises given and taken tonight before Him and those gathered here."

Leonie's hand shook as she took the ring he'd wear and kissed it before sliding it onto his hand. "Those joined here tonight, are joined forever," she murmured.

Dove responded by sliding a ring on her shaking hand. "This ring is the symbol of my faithfulness. Wear it forever in the knowledge it is freely given," he intoned.

They knelt, and he prayed for them before they rose and turned to face the small crowd.

"Meet my wife," Dove called, and they cheered.

LEONIE SAT BESIDE HIM, hand twined in his, while the festivities took place. There weren't speeches, but the meal felt like it dragged on when all Dove wanted was to be alone with his bride.

He felt her nerves in the jump of her pulse. She shifted from time to time as well.

"Are you okay?" he whispered, and she turned to him, her eyes glowing in the lamplight.

"I'm great, but I hardly know these people, and this gown is actually really uncomfortable."

He laughed, then a flash went off. He looked up to catch Elaine's grin, a tiny digital camera in her hand. "Action shot," she said with a laugh.

They lined up for a more formal portrait, and Dove wound his arm around his bride's waist.

When the small assembly of guests finally left, taking the tables and detritus, and Liam and Leroy carting the altar back into the small church, Leonie and Dove entered the house, closing the door behind them.

"Coffee?" Leonie asked, her voice strangled.

He shook his head and drew her close. "You are a beautiful bride, wife."

Something shifted inside him, filling the spaces he'd barely noted were hollow.

"You were a handsome groom." She extended her hand, sliding

her fingers over his cheek until her thumb touched his lips. "Kiss me, husband."

Leaning down so their lips would touch in a chaste kiss, he controlled the sudden urge to scoop her up and carry her to the bed. This was their first time. *His first time.* While he knew and understood the mechanics, the sudden knowledge that tonight was the time overwhelmed him.

"I'm…" He stumbled, knowing he'd have to tell her.

"It's okay, Dove. It's my first time too." She whispered the words against his mouth, and he exhaled in thankfulness.

"Then we'll explore together."

By the light of the lamps he drew her into the bedroom, turned her, and reached for the buttons of her gown. The tiny pearls numbered in the hundreds he was sure, as he carefully worked them from the lacey loops.

Her hair cascaded down, and he brushed it aside. Leonie shivered, and his breath came faster, along with the beat of his heart.

Finally, the gown slithered to the floor, and his wife stood before him, back turned, but he could see the lacey, white panties and the tiny clasps of her bra.

His fingers clenched. Should he unfasten them or wait? The moment of indecision passed as she turned, his hand resting on her waist and sliding along the miles of silky, smooth skin.

"Dove?" Her voice echoed her uncertainty.

"Beautiful." The word slipped between his lips, unbidden yet true. In the pale light, with almost all her skin uncovered, she was truly a vision. Breasts high, cupped in white, a flat belly, and hips that flared gently. Her feet were bare, toenails painted the same ruby color as her lips.

Leonie reached for him, sliding off his jacket, the only one they'd found in the store that fit, and toyed with the top button of his black dress shirt. With a flick, the button released, and he gulped.

"Is this okay?" she breathed, and he nodded, words too difficult to form right now.

She flicked another button open, then a third, and the shirt gaped.

"The rest," he said, finally pushing the words out past the strangling lump in his throat. "Do the rest."

She did, every touch tentative, while she bit her luscious lips. He had to restrain the groan that rose because she was drawing it out, making the wait seem interminable.

Once the shirt was completely open, they worked together to slip it from his shoulders. He captured her gaze with his eyes and reached for the buckle of his belt and the jeans. He toed out of his shoes, and with a thud, the pants joined the gown on the floor.

She gasped when he pulled her against him. He knew that the jutting ridge of his erection pushed against her belly was increasing their awareness of each other.

"I want you, Leonie," he whispered. "I want this to be right for you."

Her smile was hesitant. "It will be. We'll both learn together."

She leaned in, initiating a kiss that rocked him, mouths open and questing, hands moving. He reached for the clasp of her bra instinctively but simply glanced his hand over it without really thinking. He needed the pleasure of skin against skin but was unsure what to do.

Her hands toyed with the band of his underwear, then slid within, sliding down, biting deep into the flesh of his buttocks.

His body burned.

The kiss turned wild, and they moved and twisted toward the bed, then fell, collapsing to the coverlet, she atop him, and he tore his mouth from hers, chest heaving as he gulped in oxygen.

She clasped him with her legs, and he groaned. "Protection. We need…"

He scrabbled for the chest of drawers, remembering Elaine's words as she left, informing him that she'd slid condoms in there. He took a second to silently thank her then returned his attention to his bride, hand fastening around the box.

Dove handed a foil packet he'd slid from the box to Leonie, and she looked at him. "I don't know how…"

He couldn't contain the throaty laugh. "I don't either."

Carefully, he opened the packet and slid the condom from the sleeve and looked down. "I should…"

She swallowed and nodded, climbing off so he could strip away the offending underwear. She did the same with her bra and panties, then they climbed back onto the bed.

Leonie glanced down his body and smiled. "Are you taking them off?" She indicated to his socks, and he wiggled his toes.

"Oh. Sure." Leaning down, he rolled them off then settled onto the bed beside her, ardor just slightly cooled until she leaned in, breasts sliding against his chest.

It was like being struck by lightning, the flash of erotic sensation shooting through his body. His cock jerked, and he sucked in a deep, unsteady breath.

He reached out, and she moved into his embrace, the full outline of her body nestled against his.

"Can I touch you?" she asked.

He nodded, and she slid a careful finger against his belly. It clenched and he hissed.

"Does that hurt?"

He groaned again. "No. I like it. A lot."

Their lips met in a clinging kiss as their hands slid over each other's bodies. Learning the dips and hollows and what made them burn hotter. His hand found the juncture of her thighs, slipped between them, and she moaned.

"Touch me," he urged, and she did, cupping him in her hand, fingertip sliding over his head.

His fingers found the heat and the warmth, and he parted her, slid a finger along the treasure and toyed with the pearl of her clitoris. She bucked, and his mouth opened against the sensitive flesh of her neck. He kissed her as she writhed.

"Dove? Please?" Her request was broken, and he reached again for the condom.

"Help me," he grunted.

Together, they applied it, rolling it down to cover his length, and the whole time his eyes remained closed while he held onto the tiny thread of control.

Once in place, he grabbed her hips. "Leonie, once I begin, I don't think I can stop." He opened his eyes, needing her to understand, but the look on her face, the trust, reassured him.

"I don't want you to, Dove. Make love to me, husband."

They rolled so he lay flat and she sprawled over him. "I heard this was better for the woman."

He helped her to position herself atop him, legs wide as he nudged against her. She lowered herself, lip firmly between her teeth, and her gaze settled on his.

Dove felt the scalding heat first, then the sensation of opening. Leonie gasped, and he noted the tears on her lashes. "Leonie?"

"It hurts," she whispered.

He rolled her. "I don't want to hurt you."

"Please, Dove, I need you, but it hurts. Just do it."

Flexing his hips, he pushed, felt the barrier give, then was seated fully inside her body.

He held still, the unnatural stiffness of her clearing the fog of passion for an instant before his body demanded more. Without conscious thought, he moved, nudged, and she moaned. He stilled, arms quivering, body aflame but desperate to do the right thing. "Leonie?"

"Do that again, Dove. Please?"

His hips flexed again, just a little, and she gasped; there was hunger and need with a dose of confusion.

"It feels good," she whispered, and the breath whooshed from his body.

He kissed her again and moved, and this time she reciprocated, her body sliding against his, the rhythm wild and hot.

Everything changed and grew. His mind expanded as the passion and hunger drove him forward. The wilder the dance, the more he wanted, until finally the pressure grew. Leonie's fingernails dug deep into his shoulders, and she stilled. A sensation like the clenching of a warm, wet, silken glove in a rhythm sent him careening over the edge, his body demanding and taking its release.

Collapsing was all he could manage, down onto her. Both their bodies heaving with the exertion.

He closed his eyes as love flooded him, love for Leonie, and he held her tight in his arms.

Chapter 8

Leonie woke, her body aching in a very unfamiliar manner. She rolled and her body came up against another, this time warm and *naked!*

Gripping the sheet tight, she launched up in the bed to peer at the other side. The weight on her hand had her looking down and spying the rings now gracing her fingers.

Her mother's rings. Given yesterday. The gold one glinting and reminding her of the promises she and Dove had exchanged the night before.

Her face flamed as she remembered the lovemaking session that had followed their wedding. They'd had *sex*, and it had been so much more than she'd expected. The pleasure, the touch and sounds. The heat.

Dove snored softly, and she took a moment to examine him. From the top of his black hair down to the fuzz coating his chest. It formed a line burrowing below the sheet to his… Her mind shied at the word.

His shoulders were broad but not overly muscular. His face carried stubble, and in the early morning light she could see the fullness of his lips.

Interest welled inside her, but she made herself rise, head to the bathroom to find a robe to cover her nakedness.

In the kitchen on the bench she noted a basket with a note attached.

Take today. Here's your breakfast. Enjoy your honeymoon.
Elaine and Liam

Pricks of tears welled. Their kindness was almost overwhelming. Leonie made two cups of coffee and returned to the bedroom, remembering Dove preferred coffee in the morning and tea at night. She placed one mug on his bedside table then padded back to her side and carefully slid into the bed.

Dove turned, his eyes sleepy. "Where've you been?" His words were tender and joined with a smile.

"Coffee," she said and held up her mug. "Yours is on the bedside table."

He smiled. "Put your cup down so I can bid my wife good morning."

She did, and he took her in his arms and kissed her in a most satisfactory manner.

"There was a basket in the kitchen from Elaine and Liam along with a note. They said to take today."

His gaze turned thoughtful. "So, what should we do?"

"I don't know. I mean, since this all started, every day has been filled with things to do. All of a sudden we've come to a stop and I…" She blinked. "What would you like to do?"

Dove smiled. "Well, there are some things we should know about each other. Over breakfast I guess we could talk about our families and what we want from our marriage, but I have to tell you, I do want kids."

She nodded, understanding and agreeing with him. This had happened fairly quickly. She'd only known him a month and now they were married.

"I also need you to know that because I'm a priest there will be times when people call on me. Emergencies. They happen all the time, and I'm committed to—"

"I understand that, Dove. I taught at the private Catholic school, so religion and God are part of my life, so I know." She nodded, swallowing hard. "And kids too. I want them, just not yet, okay?"

He cupped her cheek. "Last night was just the beginning, Leonie. We'll make this work. I know it was quick but…"

She had the impression he hunted for the right way to describe their situation. "I know. The whole situation means we have to make our own new 'normal', and I'm okay with that."

"I also need to meet with Liam. I had a thought yesterday, and it's important."

She was sure he didn't want to alarm her. It was like he kept the thoughts—dark and scary if the shadows in his eyes were to be believed—to himself.

THEY TALKED through breakfast then Dove took her into his chapel. Leonie listened patiently as he explained what everything was and how it was used. Afterward, she showed him the books she'd brought with her and talked about the children she taught.

They'd both agreed that they needed to 'get to know each other' because they'd had so little time beforehand to do the things most couples did before marriage.

Lunch was quick, because the urgency between them grew and bloomed. He dragged her to the bedroom, and they touched and kissed until they were breathless then they fell to the bed, a tangle of limbs.

She gasped into his mouth as he plunged deep within her body. Leonie's fingers dug deep as she entreated him to give "more" in the broken whisper he adored already.

She bucked wildly beneath him, legs wound around his waist, and they exploded in each other's arms, his head flung back. "Leonie!"

Once spent, they lay in each other's arms, him caressing her face and wondering at the gift he'd received.

"I have to go back to work tomorrow." She spoke quietly, and he bent his head to hear. "The kids need me. They need routine."

He understood what she was saying. Today they could be like teenagers, but tomorrow their lives would resume, the outside an intrusion, and it reminded him that nothing was assured anymore.

The attack on the building was a concern that would have to be addressed. He very much doubted those they'd met with realized what he'd already worked out. One zombie usually meant more. If they were the mutated versions, more would come. A force of them. Stronger, faster, and more driven. Savagery like they'd never yet seen.

"Dove?" Leonie rose up in the bed, her arms encircling him, and he realized he'd been lost in thought. "What is it?"

"Not today," he said and kissed her forehead, hoping she wouldn't pursue the thoughts that chased around in his mind.

Leonie shook her head. "No. Your worries are mine too. Tell me."

He scrubbed his hands over his face. "Zombies are pack creatures. Where there's one——"

"More follow," she said as her face paled. "You think they'll come here?"

"I do. In greater numbers and strength. The one at the units was bigger and stronger. Faster. I saw his eyes. If they come, we'll be hard-pressed to stop them. The gates and walls are metal and well-made, but they're still scalable."

"Oh. My. God." Leonie folded her hands across her stomach and stared at him in horror. "If they come... We're not safe, are we?"

"I don't know, Leonie. I wish I could say we were. I wish something would happen and God would make us free of them. But I can't say that."

Helplessness was an emotion he'd tried to push away, but it swamped him. Because now it wasn't just him against the world. Leonie was too important. How could he protect her?

He gathered her close. "We make the best of it. We plan for the worst and hope for the best, Leonie. I'm not letting you go, and I'll do my best to keep you safe."

The scalding heat of her tears almost unmanned him. "I don't want to lose you, Dove. What I said last night—that I loved you—it's true. I'm afraid too, but for you I'll do my best."

Squeezing his eyes shut, Dove thanked God for this woman. She had an inner strength, and he loved her. Loved every aspect of her. Who she was as a person—honest and hardworking—among her many qualities.

Tell her, urged his psyche.

"Leonie?" He gripped her hard against his chest. "I love you." The words jumbled out, thick and urgent.

She cried, ripping sobs that left her shaking, and he wondered what he'd done. Bewildered, he held her, wanting the weeping to end and hoping he hadn't made some kind of mistake in telling her.

"Leonie? What did I do?"

She shook harder, gripped him tighter, and he waited until the storm passed. "I never thought anyone would love me. Not for me. At home I was the dutiful and quiet daughter, then the teacher. Then I became a prospective mate because I was young and likely fertile, but no one saw *me*. The person below the surface. A woman with needs and emotions. Gary took me away because I was his sister and he felt responsible. But I wanted more. I wanted to be loved for me. For who I am. I didn't think that would happen once the virus spread. I told myself it didn't matter and almost believed it. Until now. Those words, Dove? They mean so much to me."

He held her close and wondered at how giving she was, without grasping or taking. She'd been prepared to accept less, and for a moment he had to close his eyes. He'd almost taken that from her in his cowardice.

"I'm sorry I almost held it back. I didn't know. Wasn't sure, but now I am."

Leonie tugged away. "I'm pleased you waited." She swiped at her eyes. "It means more because I know you did that."

He wanted to lie there and hold her, but when he reached for her, Leonie shook her head. "No. We need to tell Liam and Elaine. It's important."

Dove wanted to argue. After all, it was their single-day honeymoon. Time for them to be alone. Together. To learn about each other. But the danger was too great for him to ignore. So instead, he climbed out of the bed and pulled on the clothes they'd discarded in their haste to once more be together in the most carnal sense.

He caught her hand in his as they made their way toward Liam and Elaine's house. Elaine sat on a seat in the living room, with Liam opposite her, holding a now sleeping baby. A large file set on the coffee table before them.

"We didn't expect to see you." Liam spoke quietly, and Dove understood it was so they didn't wake Isla.

"It couldn't wait, Liam. We need to talk." Dove settled onto a seat and waited for Leonie to do the same. He caught her close, arm around her shoulders. "We've missed something, Liam. What is the first thing we learned about zombie behavior?"

The man frowned as if thinking back to the first time he'd seen them. "They follow."

Dove nodded. "They follow. They follow humans, they follow vehicles, and they follow each other."

For a moment incomprehension settled on Liam, then something new took its place. Understanding. "They move in packs."

"Yes. Where there's one, there's more. We had a single lone one. A mutated, strong zombie." He let the words fall.

"More," said Elaine, her hands gripping together.

"Stronger. Mutated. *Shit!* We missed it. Something so fucking basic," Liam ground out, and Dove waited. "The building. He got in."

"I don't think the gates here are strong enough. A group will push. They'll be even stronger together, united. We can fight back, but I'm not sure we can be fast enough." The words burned Dove as they tumbled out, acidic and terrifying.

Liam handed the baby to Elaine then stood as the baby woke and wailed. Elaine jostled the baby with Liam stalking the room.

"How? How do we protect everyone?" He turned tortured eyes on Dove.

"Electricity. We have access to a number of electric fence devices. They might give us the time we need, but Liam, the danger is growing again. Something has to happen. We have to fight back, otherwise what has been built here is for nothing." He couldn't control the bitter disappointment and fury that hammered at him. He glanced at Leonie who waited in silence.

"You're saying that we need to come together now, fight back against the militia? We've tried that before. It didn't work, remember? You were on the mission."

Dove flinched.

"That was before. It was almost academic then, but the reality is that zombie broke into a fortified building. He would have killed everyone, Liam. Dove's right. Something has to happen." Leonie's quiet words broke the tension.

"We could call together all the heads of the communities. Most now have transport." Liam scraped his hand through his hair, clearly thinking aloud.

"For long term, I think that's wise. But we need to think immediate. What options are there?" Dove asked, and Liam slumped into a chair. His face settled into a visage of anger and fear.

Dove knew how he felt.

Leonie cleared her throat. "The people in the units aren't safe, are they? I mean they're the first place they'd attack because they don't have the protections we do."

Dove nodded. "Yes, that's true."

"How many are trained?" Her voice sounded strangled.

"Everyone has been given some basic form of self-defense training. Or the adults at least," Liam muttered, and Dove waited, wondering what she was thinking.

"We need to move the kids and mothers of the young, the elderly too, to the center. Then we put some of the strongest into rings. I'm pretty damn good with a rifle. Give me one and I'll pick them off." Leonie's voice hardened, and Dove stared at his wife.

"What?" There was no missing the strain in Dove's voice.

"I lived in the outback all my life, where there were lots of moving vermin, so I learned early on how to use a rifle. I can shoot pretty well, even take down a 'roo from seven hundred meters depending on the weapon. Kill on the first shot." Her eyes took on a hardness Dove had never seen before in her. "Anyone who can fire a rifle should be armed. Cattle prods help too. I know how to make them. Well, rudimentary ones using battery packs and iron rods."

Liam stared at her, and Dove knew the man was weighing up Leonie's comments. "What do you need, Leonie? I'll have the men hunt up the supplies. We'll organize a working party to manufacture enough to help keep us all safe."

Dove's stomach congealed. "I can't…"

"You leave the prods to me, Dove. It won't kill them, just shock them enough to give the people you're with time to get help." Her thumb rubbed over her hand where they were still twined together. "I understand, you're a priest, but I'm not. I can do this. It's okay."

LEONIE SAT DOWN, pencil in hand, an eraser to the left, and a sheet of paper. How did Gary do this? The connection to the battery—and what kind would be best—had her biting her lip.

Dove slipped a glass of cold water onto the table beside her and took up position. "So, a kindergarten teacher who can design a cattle prod, huh?"

She sighed. "Gary used to make them all the time. When the boys went out to clear toads, he'd always have a couple on hand. He'd disengage the batteries until they were required. Said it made 'dealing with them short work'." Leonie couldn't help but smile at the memory. Funny how something that really was an awful skill now reminded her of good times.

"You miss him?"

"Gary? Yeah. He was a great big brother. Kept me safe in the last couple of years. Helped me with the heavy stuff I couldn't do. Life wasn't easy, but he was there to support me." The grief she carried around felt a little lighter for talking about him. "He was awful at school. Used to tease me. His nickname for me was 'Lonely Leonie', but I knew if someone tried to pick on me, he'd be there. He could always have first jab at me, but no one else was allowed, if you know what I mean?"

"It's okay to miss him." Dove rubbed her hand.

"I know. It's been frantic since I got here though, so the time I've had…" Leonie shrugged. "I think about him. I remember how he…" Now she choked up. "…died. It was awful, but I realize I can't change it, no matter how much I wish I could."

"If you want to talk about him…" Dove's words trailed away.

"I know. I will. When this is done. I want to add his name to the remembrance tree, and my parents too. My little sister too."

"Then we shall, dearest wife." He cuddled her close, as if he was transmitting the support through touch to her.

The words and his closeness settled the nerves in her belly, and she looked down, inspiration coming in a flash as she sketched out the connector they'd need. She turned it on its side, squinting at her work. "I think that's how he did it. But if there's an electrician here about, he can take a look and maybe tweak it a little. Gary wasn't trained properly, he just learned on the job for when we couldn't get someone to do the electrical work." On a sigh, she sat back and glanced at the clock.

"We're eating at the refectory tonight. Liam has organized a meeting of the board to explain what we've learned."

Dove rose and she shook her head. "Then I'll stay here."

"No. Liam wants you there to explain the prod. We need you there. I want you there, with me." He held out his hand, and she accepted it. "Bring your plans with you. They'll want to see them."

They left the house and walked up the path to the large shed filled with long tables and bench seats. A group of people gathered at the far table, Liam, Elaine, and little Isla in the center.

The familiar 'I don't belong here' jumble of nerves started to remind her she was an interloper, and to be honest, she would have run if not for the steadying force of Dove's hand.

He took up a spot at the table, making sure there was room for her too, and he introduced her to those gathered around. Some she'd already met, but the majority were new to her. Old and young, the group was a cross section of their adult community.

"You said it's urgent," one of the older ladies said, her white hair ruthlessly short, but her eyes keen as she pinned Liam who placed the large file Leonie had seen on the coffee table in front of him.

"I've got some interesting and worrying information. Based on the intelligence we've managed to get hold of, if we account for every known and captured zombie and allow for the loss in economics, each would have cost the economy somewhere in the region of six million dollars." Liam settled back in his seat, eyes glinting with a mix of fury and humor.

Leonie blinked. "What? Who has time to consider that?" The words slipped out, but the ripple of laughter at the table cleared some of the fraught emotions that had been present before.

"Yeah, well, that came from Anterrum, but I'm not sure where he got it from. Must be some leftover boffin from before the zombies." Liam grinned then settled his mirth. "We should begin."

Mugs settled on the table as the hub of chatter died away.

"Dove and Leonie made some observations. He saw a group of mutated zombies and said they were headed our way. Then there was the attack on the units yesterday." Liam's words hit her right between the eyes. Just yesterday she'd been in the building, and then they had married and she'd…

Someone else was speaking, and she had to push through the veil of unreality to focus.

"Okay?" Dove spoke quietly to her, and she nodded.

"Anyway, they think he was like an advance scout. They'll follow soon. And in big numbers. We don't know exactly how many there are," Liam finished.

"But you said Dove saw them?" the older woman questioned.

Dove cleared his throat. "We know they hunt in packs. They don't always converge until they find a patch of meat. Particularly humans. I'm of the opinion the ones I saw are still the front of the pack. More will come, and we know, categorically now, that they're stronger. More capable. Far more dangerous." He waited as some shifted in the chairs, and Leonie watched them, noting the hard glints in more than one gaze.

"So, what do you suggest?" a grizzled man demanded. "We have to be able to protect those inside the community."

Dove nodded. "I agree. We electrify the fences, bring everyone back here so we're contained in one location and we aren't splitting the guards. We move the youngest and oldest to the center of the camp. They're a draw to the zombies, so we fortify their location as much as we can."

A man to her left scratched his head. "But when? When do we expect them?"

Liam shrugged. "We could send out teams to see what they can find out, but then we're opening ourselves up needlessly. We have already put lookouts on buildings around to alert us, but it's like asking how long is a piece of string. We don't know until they're coming into our sights."

"So, they break through the barriers. Then what? They pick off those who can shoot and the others are left defenseless." A woman's voice quivered with fright, and Leonie didn't want to know who said the words. It made it sound all too real.

"Concentric circles." Liam's voice was infinitely patient. "We form circles. Put some of our best shots on roofs ready to start as soon as they breach the barriers. For closer in, Leonie here, had an idea for cattle prods. We make our own. Use them to herd the zombies away from our most vulnerable. Into a secure location. Somewhere we can deal with the threat."

With shock, Leonie turned back to Liam. His face was hard though pale, and beads of sweat coursed down the sides of his cheeks.

She wanted to ask what that meant exactly. Would they kill the zombies? But Dove nudged her and prompted, "Go ahead."

With a jerky nod, she held up the design she'd not long finished. "I think we could customize some rods, electrify them so we can deliver a shock. It will probably need to be a fair jolt, but it will move them away from those we're protecting." She pointed to the handle. "This area here is insulated so we don't get injured while using it. We connect a very basic battery pack, and each time the connection makes contact…*zap*."

They leaned forward, and Liam requested that she send the sheet around the table. One man at the end, grizzled and leather-skinned, nodded as he inspected the design. "I can see the rudiments. We've got everything needed in the electrical store. I can whip some up in no time. We can test them pretty quickly."

Liam exhaled. "That's great. How soon do you think you could have the first put together?"

The man shrugged. "It's a basic design, and I can put together a prototype maybe tonight even."

The group agreed that tomorrow morning was a wise time for Leonie to attend the workshop to see the testing of the prod.

"Where do we drive them to?" another called from further down the table, and the conversation turned to the number of empty containers dotted around the grounds for storing things in.

"That would do nicely in the short term," Ramon said. "Until they can be dealt with."

Liam cleared his throat. "Dove also pointed out that now is the time to deal with the threat of the mutated zombies. We can guess the militia are behind it. When Julia and Leroy took the team out last year, we learned they were gathering them up. Experimenting. Dove and his team also brought back valuable intelligence, but they're massing. We need help. External assistance. Now is the time to bring in the other camp commanders. Look to forge alliances."

"The last time we tried that they refused. What makes you think they'll get involved now?" asked the white-haired lady who'd spoken earlier.

"The tests Ramon has been running are conclusive." Liam spread his hands, seeking their agreement. "The injured guard also doesn't appear to be changing, so we can conclude these mutated zombies are only meant to be tools to clear the communities. Send them in, clear the place…"

Once again Dove entered the discussion. "We need assistance if we're going to beat it. We need access to the outside world. To do that, we need everyone working together. With assistance from the outside, we can reclaim our country. Our remaining scientists have been working for a long time to find a vaccine. But we all know, once turned, these zombies can't be salvaged. So we must clear them." He grimaced as if the words caused him pain. They probably did, because she knew it was against his beliefs to kill.

The meeting rolled around ideas and plans, yet nothing conclusive was decided until the end when Liam raised his hand, ending the conversations that flowed and the arguments that ensued. He waited for silence to descend on the table.

"We need to make a decision. Here and now. Do we address the other communities? Ask for their input and assistance? For those who vote yes, raise your hands."

Slowly, hands raised as if it was the most difficult decision in the world to make. *It probably was*, she thought. Effectively, they were deciding whether they should go to war, not continuing the skirmishes they'd lived with over the last few years.

"And those who don't think this is the best idea."

One hand. A second. Silence stretched like a cord pulled tight, then the pressure snapped.

"I guess we have a decision then," Liam said. "Elaine and I will be in contact with the other camp commanders. Invite them here to discuss what's going on."

The group broke up until only the five of them—Elaine, Liam and their daughter, herself and Dove—remained at the table.

Leonie wondered if they should they leave, but a woman came closer, bearing plates of the chicken stew that seemed to form a great part of their diet. She slid the plates in front of them one by one, added cutlery, then melted away.

"Dove, you're the voice of reason on the board. While we're busy with the negotiations, Elaine and I agree you would be the best person to take on the day-to-day responsibility for the community."

He jolted upright and she reached for his hand, which vibrated. "I'm not sure I'm the right—"

"Nonsense," said Elaine, leaning forward. "You have the respect of those in the camp. You've always demonstrated sensible thought processes, and the board trusts you. We discussed it before you arrived, and we all agree. So consider it done."

"I'm…overwhelmed."

He smiled though and it heartened her. After that the dinner was almost silent as they ate then left.

She slid her hand into his, enjoying the breeze that caressed her. Near the door, he stopped her, turned her under the moonlight so she could see his face. "I'm at sea, Leonie. I don't know how to lead these people."

"Everything Liam and Elaine said is right, Dove. I've seen the way they defer to you. You would never put someone in harm's way. You won't allow people to do things that are wrong. All facets of an excellent leader." Rising onto tiptoe, she kissed him and felt the burn of the heat in her belly. The flare of passion and need that was ever present.

He tugged away on a curse. "Inside, Leonie. Now." The depth of his voice and the sudden hardness of his body betrayed his own arousal, and she smiled.

"Of course, husband."

Chapter 9

Dove slammed the door shut behind them, feeling the pounding of blood in his veins.

His wife stood before him, Leonie's cheeks pink and her eyes shining with the answer to his passion. Her lips, swollen from the fast and damned hot kiss, urged him to move toward her.

Taking her in his arms, he tugged her close to his body, aware that his erection nudged against the softness of her belly.

His fingers shook as he reached for the buttons of the light shirt she wore. He fumbled. "Damn it!" The shaking made his movements uncoordinated and clumsy.

Leonie laughed, a throaty sound, and shoved his hands away. "Let me do that. I like this shirt." She undid the top buttons before sliding it off and over her head.

He gazed his fill, noting the soft mounds of her breasts in the lacey bra and the way they'd taken on a rosy tinge, while her eyes turned slumberous.

"I want you." His words filled the air, and she smiled, her lips flicking up at the corners.

"I know." And she winked, the minx!

Her hands found the clasp of his belt.

"Shirt first?" he suggested.

She giggled. "Why be conventional?" The tongue of the belt came free, and she jerked it from his jeans.

"In that case…" he murmured and stripped her of her shorts and panties.

She fumbled with the button and zipper on his jeans and they dropped as he caught her up and moved her back against the door. The kiss they shared ignited him.

Passion oozed from every pore as they moved against each other. Her legs swung around his waist and she opened for him, parted so he could slide his hard, aching cock deep inside her. He felt the glove of her, hot and welcoming.

She cried out, and his lips moved to the tender spot on her neck. "Oh, Dove, I love you," she crooned as they undulated. Neither action soft or gentle, but instead savage and hungry. Demanding.

Thrusting and undulating, they rode the passion as if their lives depended on it.

His mind told him to slow down, but his body demanded every ounce of her, everything she had to give, and the pressure mounted deep in his body. The need to claim and love her forever the driving force.

"For me, Leonie," he demanded as she stiffened and called his name on a broken cry released into the air.

His body jammed her one last time against the door as he spilled himself deep inside her.

Breathing harshly, he rested his forehead against hers and took a moment to enjoy the aftermath before reality intruded.

"Oh God, Leonie. I didn't hurt you, did I?"

Her eyes looked unfocused, and she gazed at him, her lips parted. "No. That was…" She gulped, still as breathless as he was. "That was amazing. I'm not sure I can move though, and if I did…" She gasped. "I don't think my legs will hold me up."

Disengaging himself from her was like tearing a limb from his body, but he hefted her in his arms as she squeaked and carried her to the bedroom. They removed the rest of their clothes and slid into the bed, with her cradled against his side.

His gaze settled on the condom pack he'd left on the bedside table, and his gut suddenly churned. "We didn't use a condom," he said. *How will she react?*

She jerked beside him then settled back into his embrace, all soft and warm. "Oh well. What's done is done."

Her words surprised him. "What's done is done?"

She shrugged. "We both agreed we want kids. I believe in the sanctity of life, and I know you do too. So, whatever happens, we're both on the same page."

Dove couldn't believe she was so welcoming already of the chance, but he embraced her answer.

In the moonlight he said a quick prayer of thanks then let the waves of slumber claim him.

LEONIE WOKE early and wondered if she should round the children up for their lessons or… Then she remembered she'd agreed to head to the electronics workshop to work on the prototype for the zombie prod, as she'd renamed it.

Dove slept silently and she gazed at him. "Dove, the children will be expecting me, but I have to…"

He rolled over and woke slowly, his eyes opening to half-mast. His grin warmed her all the way to her belly. "Good morning, wife."

Oh, the sound of that is like a million Christmas mornings and presents all rolled into one great big surprise.

She leaned in, aware of her nakedness but more comfortable than the morning before, but still she clutched the sheet against her breasts.

Dove reached out and gently tugged the material. "You don't need this, Leonie. Not between you and I. Whatever we do together, we both consent to. But if you are… If you need me to stop, just say the words and I will."

She released the fabric and let it fall away, displaying her nakedness to Dove's gaze. "I know, it just still feels odd."

His hand settled on her shoulder and pulled her in for a gentle kiss, and when they broke away, she felt complete and at peace.

"I'm not sure how to let the kids know I won't be there today. I'm supposed to meet with the men at the electronics hut, but I don't want to let the kids down. It wouldn't be right."

Dove made a sound in his throat that she guessed was agreement. "I can swing around and let them know, if you like."

I'm so lucky. "That would be great, if it's not getting in the way of your plans."

"No, not at all. Besides, it's only just dawn and we've got time." He waggled his eyebrows in what she guessed he thought was a suggestive manner, and she couldn't contain her giggle.

"No. We need to get up and ready for the day."

On a hard-done-by groan he rose, and she took a moment to watch him. Grace and fluidity married with a naked torso and firm ass. The vibrating sound of pleasure erupted, and he turned, spied her watching him.

"Like what you see?" His eyes burned, and heaven help her, the place between her legs, the one that grew moist at the thought of him, started doing its thing.

"I do. Very much." *Who wouldn't?* she thought, her gaze traveling the length of his body, stopping on his engorged penis.

Seconds passed, long and heavy with desire, stealing the oxygen from her lungs and making her want.

"Leonie?"

She blinked, coming out of the stupor and realizing he was watching and waiting.

"Dove, I want you, but what about…"

Sinking back down onto the bed, he took her in his arms, their lips meeting and clinging. "We have responsibilities, I know. But the first one is to those at home. You're my home, Leonie. Wherever you are is where I belong. Where my most important responsibilities lie."

Cupping his face, she read only honesty in his eyes. "I believe you. But lives depend on us."

Dove's sigh broke the spell, and he tugged away. "You're right.

We should eat then go about our business. The thing is, we can't panic. That will cause more issues than it solves, so we must remain calm in our demeanor."

Leonie reached for some clothes and dressed quickly, *tsking* as she entered the lounge and noted the discarded garments from the night before. As she bent to collect them, Dove beat her to it, scooping them up and carrying them to the hamper in the bathroom.

As she moved about, putting on the kettle, grabbing some bread to toast over the stove top, she wondered how other communities managed. Did they have the kind of setup like this camp had?

Before they could sit down to eat, a knock came at the door and the calling of Dove's name. The urgency in the tone was unmistakable, and with a quick glance in her direction, Dove moved to the door and pulled it open.

On the other side, she spied Leroy. "Liam sent for you. Two more zombies have been located on the edge of the community, and they're trying to get in."

She hurried out the door after the two men as they dashed to Liam's house, and she entered mere steps behind them. Already a group of people had gathered, including Julia "Good, you're here," Liam said. "The southern boundary is seeing an attempt from two zombies. Large and strong. They've tried to push through the fence. They haven't breached it, but this is the validation of what you said. We need to get things moving. Set the plans in place."

Elaine came bolting down the stairs, a small bag flung over her shoulder and the babe in her arms.

"Elaine will go with you to the school and hospital. We're going to set up a base for families of young children who require their parents, older children up to twelve, the aged, and those unable to fight. Leroy, you're to head their guards. Dove, work with Elaine to formulate a list. We need to know who is where, in case the worst happens. Leonie, I need you over at the stores. We're rounding up the trained guards now."

Leonie understood the importance of her role, but being sent away from Dove terrified her. A yawning pit of frozen ice invaded her bones. "I understand." She turned, but before she could leave, Dove kissed her. Hard and demanding.

"Whatever happens, keep safe. I'll find you later," Dove growled.

It was a promise, a vow, and Leonie sent up a quick prayer of her own for their safety before leaving him behind.

DOVE WATCHED LEONIE GO. Saw that she squared her shoulders, and his heart ached for both of them. Would this be the last time they saw each other? In his mind, he knew that this was the beginning of a dangerous time. Survival wasn't assured, and the thought that they would be separated left his soul screaming with anguish.

He turned and saw Liam's gaze. Read the concern and understanding.

"We need to get moving. I take it that's Isla's things?" He motioned to the bag, and Elaine nodded, her eyes shining with moisture.

"Yeah. I have the full list of everyone in the camp here." She rushed to the filing cabinet and caught Liam's eye. Dove indicated that he'd leave and walked out of the house to wait just beyond in the garden.

When Elaine emerged, she dabbed at her eyes, streaks on her cheeks betraying the tears she'd shed. He reached for the bag and they moved swiftly, heading toward the old school which was now converted to a hospital and reception area. An older building, it had been retro-fitted to fulfill the needs of the community, but once more, its use would change to a shelter for those unable to protect themselves.

Ramon met them at the stairs, his face hard. "Liam's not coming?"

Elaine shook her head. "He's trying to contact all the commanders, but we're going to bring in the youngsters, because things have changed, Ramon. Here, take your niece." She handed the baby to

Liam's brother and surged inside, the emotional woman replaced by one with a mission.

"What does she mean?" Ramon juggled the baby who'd started to babble.

"We'll tell you inside, but time is of the essence, friend."

They headed into the building, and Dove didn't turn back, even though he wanted to.

They settled in Ramon's office, the chair squeaking as Dove sank into it, and they quickly explained what Dove had shared the night before, the ramifications. The plan for protection. And Ramon's face grew grimmer and more drawn by the moment.

"I understand what you're saying, but here we've got the injured, pregnant, and laboring."

Dove rubbed his hand across his brow. "This is the most secure location. The best place to bring those who can't fight. We can use the upstairs for families and children. The women and older will look after them. We'll stay out of the way."

"My wards…"

"Ramon, we have nowhere else to go. If they break through the fences, no one will survive," Elaine summed up the situation, and Ramon closed his eyes, pinching the bridge of his nose.

"Keep my theatre free and the consult rooms. I can use them for triage as required." He looked at the window and exhaled. "I need my staff." He rose jerkily, but Dove reached out and grabbed the man's hand.

"Take a moment, Ramon. While we can. Elaine and Isla will stay here, and Leroy is coming as the defense coordinator for this area. I'm about to head out and round up those who need to come."

"We need some supplies. Water, food, bedding," Ramon mumbled, and Dove agreed.

"While I'm on my rounds, I'll set that up. They will be arriving as soon as I can get them mobile."

Dove rose and stepped out into the fresh air. Around him, people went about their business, unaware that later today they'd be mobilized, their lives about to be upended once again. All because of the machinations of men with no understanding or interest in the damage their evil plans would wreak.

He jammed his hands into the pockets of his jeans, wondering how Leonie was faring. If she too felt the wave of fear that swirled deep inside him.

Dove turned and headed out, because wishing and hoping wasn't going to save anyone, least of all, the two of them.

———

LEONIE'S STOMACH knotted as she entered the work area. The elderly man waited for her and took a look at whatever emotion he could read on her face.

"What's happened?" he asked.

She splayed her hands. "Two zombies have attacked the corner of the community. Liam needs the prods ready now. So, I'm here and we need to see what we can do to get enough manufactured. I guess… Do you have any apprentices or kids who'd be useful? Once we get the first one made, we can create a production line."

The grizzled man stared at her. "I got a few. Let me send my wife out. She knows where they are."

He left Leonie staring at the rows of metal and conduit cords hanging here and there. It was as if Gary were there with her, and without thought, she moved forward, collecting what she knew he'd always chosen.

Every move was unconscious, but before she knew it, the items were laid out and her hands moving. Creating the connector was simple as she jury-rigged an old torchlight's connectors and the large, squat battery. Next came the conduit to carry the charge to the rod. She stripped and wound the wires to make a stable connection. The insulation she added to the rod was in the form of tape, and she wound it tight, secured it just as the old man returned.

His eyes widened, checking out the prod she'd just created. "Well now, that's probably effective, but if we replace the insulation tape for flexible piping, it might be more comfortable."

Leonie jumped. "Oh, sorry." She stepped away, and he shook his head.

"No, what you've created is workable. We can make them quickly with the equipment on hand. Grab as many of everything as you can. The boys are on their way."

With a nod, Leonie set to work, assembling the parts as he joined her, each made up into sets so the task would be completed quickly.

As the 'boys' arrived Leonie started showing them how to assemble the prods. One suggested a different way to make the connection of wire to rod, and they found it was not just more effective, but faster to create as well as more reliable.

The others caught on quickly, their hands faster than hers at completing the tasks. By the time the sun was high in the sky an impressive pile of completed prods lay by the door.

Biting her lip, Leonie wondered how many of these devices would see action. They tested each one, looking for the spark, and while some were discarded, the majority of them were shuffled into black plastic containers to be carried over to the hospital.

They stopped for lunch, but even after they returned her mind was only half on the task, the other seeking any sign of Dove. The silence strangled her. Where was he? Was he okay?

Dusk was hazing the horizon when he appeared, his face drawn and eyes ringed with shadows. "Dove?"

"It's okay. We should go home. Arrangements are being made for this evening, but we're free tonight, unless there's some kind of attack. The sharpshooters are going tonight to find their locations where they can watch and see, under the cover of dark. They'll alert the guards if they see anything we need to know about. They've all been allocated walkie-talkies we found, so we'll hear quickly enough."

He wound his arm around her and pulled her close. She inhaled the scent of him and gloried in the strength of this man. *My husband.* Trudging home, she breathed deeply and considered how to make her request.

"Dove, I'm a good shot. With a rifle, I'll be useful."

He stopped and looked at her, his beautiful blue eyes wide with startlement. "What?"

"I'm used to shooting. I did mention it. Give me a rifle and let me help with the defense."

"I…"

She knew it was hard for him to come to terms with her request. Surely, no priest ever thought his mate would be in this position. She didn't want it, but she felt keenly the responsibility she had to everyone around her.

"No." The word came out garbled.

"Yes," she insisted. "I have to do this, Dove. You can't fight, and I understand that. Under normal circumstances, neither could I, but I have to under these circumstances."

It hurt her to see the warring emotions on his face, but he had to understand. Acknowledge where she was coming from.

"I see." He turned away, and it gutted her.

"What do you understand?" Constriction narrowed her throat.

"I'll make the arrangements." He sounded remote, and heaven help her, right now she didn't know what to say. The truth was she had so little understanding of how he thought in unusual situations. Maybe that was because they barely knew each other before they'd agreed to marry.

"Dove?" Her voice was barely a whisper and uncertain.

His face was pale when he turned back. "It's okay, Leonie. I know this is me, but I just want you safe."

Her heart clenched, because there was a terrible vulnerability in his eyes.

Leonie reached out. "Tell me."

"At home," he said and took her hand.

They walked in silence through the door, and once it closed behind them, he settled them both on the lounge chair, his arm wound around her waist.

"I was at a school. A private one on the outskirts of Canberra itself. A girl's school," he said. "When the call went out, we locked down. Tried to keep the girls safe, but you probably know what it was like."

The cold remoteness in his voice, the stiff way he held himself, interspersed with shivers now and then, froze her to the core.

"No, not really," she said. "I mean, we had some come into the area. But it wasn't like here, but we saw coverage for a while… As long as the television stations were broadcasting, we heard what was going on. Then we had travelers arrive, the sort who were running away from the cities. Some of them brought it with them." *I'm babbling*, she thought.

Dove shook his head, as if trying to clear the memories from his mind. "It was horrific. They came in droves. Hundreds breaking through the gates. We holed up as best we could, but they picked them off, the kids and staff. One by one. I heard the screams. I pulled some girls into the church with me. I didn't know until later one of them had been bitten. She turned and killed the rest in the middle of the night. They were in the office. I was in the sacristy next door. Opened it when I heard it all, but it was too late. So, I locked the door and hid." His voice broke on the final word.

Dove broke down, the paroxysms tearing at him.

She dragged him close and slipped her arms around him, holding tight. "You did everything you could. You tried to protect them, but if I've learned nothing else, it doesn't matter what you do. If they're determined, they'll find a way. I'm thankful you're still here, Dove."

"I don't… I feel sometimes, like I'm so *unworthy*." He turned away, as if ashamed to show his grief. "They died, and they were innocent. Just children. I saw some of them later, while we were in the city on a mission. The uniforms and what they'd become. They were little more than animated corpses, and yet I couldn't give them peace. Last rites was all I could manage. It doesn't feel like I've done enough."

Her heart cracked. "No, you did. I'll bet the people with you gave them that?"

He nodded, face still averted.

"In peace, with the blessings you called for them, they will find rest. Dove, you have to understand that it wasn't your fault. The same as it's not now. Guilt is part of grief, but you have to allow yourself to feel it in order for your soul to heal."

"But you want to put yourself at risk!"

Such stark fear in his voice ripped at her soul. Launching herself to the ground, she sank to her knees, gripping his face in her hands. "Listen to me, Dove. I'm afraid. You're afraid. That's okay. If we weren't, we'd be stupid, and that's something neither of us is. But I have to do this, just like you have to be there with those in the hospital. You have a role—an important one—the same as I do. I can fight, but you're there giving care. Helping Ramon and keeping it all together for us. Once we succeed, and I have to hope we do, everyone is going to need the skills you offer, and that's no mean feat."

Was it enough? Would he understand she wasn't just talking?

His face was wet with tears, and she slid into his embrace.

"I'm just afraid to lose you, Leonie. You understand what I'm feeling." He gave an embarrassed laugh. "Even when I'm talking like a wimp."

The tiny hint of humor settled the nerves jumping about her belly, and she exhaled. "We need a shower and some food. Then the best thing we can do is head to bed. Sleep deep because tomorrow will be another busy day."

They rose, and he led her to the bathroom. They dragged, physically and emotionally drained, but stepping into the shower, which delivered hot, soothing water, Leonie took a moment to let it revive her low spirits.

Once cleansed, she stepped from the stall and into his arms, and the towel he held for her. Wrapping it around herself, she followed him to the bedroom where they threw on comfortable clothes. Leggings and a t-shirt for her, and trackpants and a t-shirt for him. Without saying a word, they understood this would be sensible in case they were summoned tonight.

Their dinner was light, just toast and eggs, then they retired.

In the darkness, they lay together, Leonie absorbing the information and shocks of the day, considering his words. She heard him whispering and knew he prayed. She closed her eyes and sent up her own, hoping for some divine assistance, because they'd need that just as much as the careful planning she guessed he and Liam had engaged in during the day.

When sleep came, it was restless, filled with dreams of red eyes in the night, hands scrabbling for her, and the sight of her brother. *"It'll be okay, Leo. Trust Dove and yourself. You'll make it through."*

DOVE WOKE, unrefreshed and nervous. He slid from the bed, not wanting to wake Leonie straight away. She slept deeply, though he knew it hadn't been restful, having woken more than once during the night as she thrashed and cried out. At those points, he comforted her, holding her in his arms and absorbing the fact that only in sleep did she seem to lose the iron hard control she'd shown during the day.

He set about making tea, his stomach too knotted for coffee this morning, and settled on the stool.

Understanding that he'd let his emotions get the better of him the day before was hard to come to terms with. The fact that he'd broken down in front of Leonie galled him. His father had taken great pains during his teen years to reinforce that 'men must always have a stiff upper lip,' but that training had clearly failed him when he'd needed inner strength most.

He sipped the tea and wondered how the day would proceed. Would they be attacked? Would there be a lull?

How did the men in the war cope? They'd displayed great bravery when under fire, but the periods of calm before the storm they had to know what was coming, or at least have an idea what to expect. His flock, as he now thought of them, needed the strength he projected, but how did he achieve this?

He cupped his chin and stared. The basics they could manage: food, shelter, and medical attention if required. But what else?

The legend of the Anzacs were drilled into children and adults before the zombie apocalypse. His mind settled to that. Memories of what he'd learned at school. The cricket and football games. The Anzac biscuits and camaraderie. Could they re-create that here?

Sliding from the chair, he jerked upright as the toll of the bells caught his attention.

The bedroom door flung open, and Leonie emerged. "Where?"

He met her at the door to the house, squeezed her hand. "Stay safe. Go straight to the farm shed. They're handing out rifles, munitions, and your prods there."

Leonie's gaze met his. "Stay safe, my love. We have years ahead of us."

At that, she took off for the shed, and he carefully closed the door to their house before heading for the old school. He had a job to do, and he'd do it to the best of his abilities.

Chapter 10

Her feet slipped, but Leonie kept running. They were coming. It was a thrum in her veins. A refrain that battered her brain, scratching against her skull.

Joining the line at the shed, she waited for a rifle. Taking a moment to make sure it wasn't loaded, she scooped up the box of rounds they shoved at her and moved aside. The men handing out the munitions didn't speak a word, just indicated she head to another man with a clipboard.

"Range?" he demanded.

"I can take seven hundred meters and a moving target."

He blinked. "Head to the main singles accommodation. They need shooters like you."

Then he turned to the next person and she moved, not at a run because that wasn't safe, but a quick pace. She reached the building and saw the small group huddled around the ladder.

Taking her turn, she followed them up, past the first and second storey to the top. *Thank God for the flat roof.* She set herself up in a corner with a clear view, the small box on the floor beside her. With trembling fingers, Leonie filled the cartridge.

It wasn't long before she caught sight of a herd of zombies.

Perhaps forty or fifty. The noise of them traveled before them. The groans and moans sending a skitter of ice down her body.

Lifting the rifle, she used the sight to follow their path. Chose one then squeezed the trigger, heart pumping. The recoil hit against her shoulder, a blinding *thwack*, but she absorbed it, checking through the raised knobs at the end of the muzzle. She'd missed.

Cursing herself, she exhaled. Then she squeezed the trigger once again.

She saw the zombie jerk as she hit the center of its head. The plume of dark blood and gray matter spewing.

It wavered, and for a moment, frustration bit deep, then the creature shuddered and fell.

Another batch must have entered. She could hear them, the din filling the air, more strident than the first group. She noted them charging forward from another direction, and Leonie cursed, her mind trying vainly to follow the second group.

She swore loud and inventively. "Who's on the second group?" Her scream went out, a cry in the commotion.

Voices called out in the affirmative.

She quickly refilled the cartridge and inserted it before redoubling her efforts. Leonie searched for another and watched as the groups spread and fractured, seeking targets within the settlement.

Other groups were dotted around the community, she knew, but terror urged her on. Another came and she struck. Two more fell before her until she noted another batch. "More incoming!"

A sound, low growling, took her by surprise, and she swung, noting one hand scrabbling at the top of the ladder. "We're under attack!"

Her bellow paid off as several on the roof turned and scanned. Multiple shots echoed in the air, loud cracks.

The gray hand raised, a head appearing over the edge, and she screamed, sighted, and squeezed the trigger.

Fright kept her frozen as the creature fell. Someone moved forward, seizing the ladder and hauling it up. "Help me," the grizzled man called even as he heaved. Others moved, assisting with the lifting until the feet of the ladder slid over the edge and the men lifting moved along the roofline.

They lay it across the roof and returned to their vantage points. She noted the wave heading past them into the center of the community and calculated how many shots were left, unloaded the cassette-like case with more bullets, then slid it back in place.

"Nooo!" The howl escaped her lips, and she moved to the other side of the building. Lifting and firing. Over and again, taking another one down, then a second from this side.

Things quieted in their area after that, and she sank to the metal roof, realizing she was soaked to the skin and the heat of the sun reflecting from the ridged material beneath her feet burned.

Someone pressed a bottle into her hand. "Drink," they ordered, and she did, letting the water soothe the burn of her parched throat.

"We didn't get them all," she whispered as she considered the situation.

"We were never going to, Leonie. We are but a single line of defense. There are others, and they'll do their part. The buildings are closer together, meaning more and more will be able to do their bit. The zombies don't have anywhere to go where they won't face our defenses."

Now she had time to think, wondering where Dove was and whether he was safe. With time to consider, the shudders and fright took root and tears burned her cheeks. *Keep him safe, God.* Of course, she had no control now and had to wait it out, just like everyone else. That came close to destroying her.

ANXIETY LEVELS RAN high in the building as Dove paced back and forth. Shots had been reported on the edges of the settlement. He wondered, not for the first time, where Leonie was. Was she safe? Then an enquiry would be directed his way and he would turn his attention to it, but the question gnawed at him all day long.

The waiting was difficult as men, women, and children huddled upstairs in the old school rooms, which had been converted to wards. He'd asked them to remain as quiet as possible, but the wail of infants, picking up on the heightened emotions, was unmistakable.

Peering out between the curtains he had demanded be closed, anxiety had his skin crawling. It felt like they'd been cowering here for hours. Glancing at the clock on the wall, he was reminded it was nearly midday. His guts gurgled, but he ignored it, keeping his eyes trained on the horizon.

The men and women had worked like trojans yesterday, putting pits and barriers in the way so they could funnel the attackers to a central location where a couple of old containers had been cleared for an enclosure.

Then he heard them. Not many, he hoped, but the sudden din hushed those huddling in the building.

He heard a cry, then the sound of gunfire. He hoped they kept the children away from the windows. He'd ordered them to keep the kids low, but children could be unpredictable.

A hand reached up, clawed at the glass, then red and gray spattered over the window and the monster reared back, and the nails scratched their way down before dropping.

Thud. Thwack. Thud. The sounds continued, and he looked over his shoulder. Dozens of gazes settled on his.

They'd agreed that no one should head outside until one of their people gave the *all clear*, but waiting proved difficult.

Time passed and silence reigned. They waited longer until suddenly a knock came at the door. With shaking legs, Dove moved forward, turned the old-fashioned key, and opened it.

Leroy entered. "We've got them, I think. Some casualties are on their way now. We've lost people too. Some bitten and others." The man shrugged, though he looked haunted by what had occurred.

Dove nodded, the dread that his wife might be one of the lost stealing his breath and slowing his heart rate. "Leonie?"

"Don't know. Waiting to hear from Julia too." Leroy's voice took on a scratchy quality, and Dove nodded, well aware of the sheer terror that they shared.

"We'll hear soon." *How I hope that's true.* He dragged the man inside. "Have a drink."

Leroy shook his head, and Dove gripped the large man's hand. "I don't think I can stomach anything right now."

He could sympathize. "Then at least sit down."

His friend blinked. "I need to get back outside. But just in case we're wrong, keep everyone inside for a little longer. Liam said he'd be around to give the *all clear* when he was sure."

Liam and a couple of sharpshooters had climbed into the carefully reinforced commodore wagon earlier in the day. He'd make rounds and bring back the wounded for Ramon and his crew to do their best with. So, all they could do was wait for him to either radio in or the vehicle to arrive. That, of course, was surmising they weren't overpowered.

The roar of an engine caught Dove's attention. "Stay inside. Lock the door after me," he called and headed outside in time to see the ugly orange vehicle, the remains of the taxi light on top smashed. Smears of blood and other stuff he didn't want to consider coated the steel plates they'd screwed on. But he saw Liam at the wheel. On the back seat sat guards, coated in blood. "Get people out here to help the wounded," he bellowed, and men and women who'd waited for his call exited the school and flooded the car.

Dove stepped back and let them go about their business as Liam clambered out.

"What a mess," Liam uttered, and Dove waited for more information. It wasn't forthcoming and the knowledge scoured him.

"Did we get them?" Dove demanded, and Liam stared.

"Yeah. But we have losses and injuries. Some got through and onto the roofs. They've not just mutated, some seem to have rational thought. They knew to climb. Had the motor skills to do that."

Fury leached from Leroy, and the boulder in Dove's belly grew. "Leonie? Julia?"

"Don't know," answered Liam as Dove's frustration and concern grew. "We'll ring the bell soon and they'll come in. We'll also need volunteers to go out and clean up."

Dove nodded. "We can organize that once we get all the people back."

Liam smiled. "True."

Dove's stomach gurgled again.

"Sounds like we should organize food right now," Liam said, and Dove frowned. "Your stomach is betraying you, friend."

How could it, in the middle of all this chaos and while he waited to see if his wife had survived? Surely that had to take priority? "I'll get food out for the men and women as they return."

As he spun on the ball of his foot, Liam grabbed his shoulder. "Don't buy trouble, friend. Our losses aren't large. I'm sure both of the women are safe." Then Liam marched past him and met his wife, who'd flown down the stairs with baby in arms to embrace her husband.

Dove sent up a prayer, hoping it would hold him until Leonie appeared, then set about arranging food.

The bells tolled, indicating that the emergency over, and he waited as people dribbled in. Others went out, tool kits in hand, the reserve guards following them to ensure their safety. They'd repair the fencing and fortifications before nightfall.

The radio behind him squawked to life and he stilled, hoping for the best but expecting the worst. "Counterpoint One. This is Counterpoint Two. Can you hear me?"

Leroy settled to the radio. "Yeah, what's the status?"

"Looking good. That was a big number, and we think it was the main pack." The voice scratched and the signal faded in and out, but the message remained clear, and a cheer went up from all around the unit.

Dove's shoulders slumped, and he ran a shaking hand over his head.

"Dove?" He heard a voice calling and turned as Julia hurried inside. He glanced over her shoulder, seeking Leonie.

"Leonie?" he said, and Julia shrugged in response, then caught sight of her husband, Leroy, and hurried forward with a wide grin on her face.

Once more Dove paced, glancing now and then over the guards

trooping in. *"Where is she?"* The words escaped in a hiss, tension oozing from every sound.

Suddenly, she was there, pale and tired, moving slowly.

His heart stuttered in his chest. He ran to her, caught her in this embrace, and slid trembling fingers over her frame. "Are you okay?" Terror gnawed at him.

She nodded, then her face screwed up and sobs erupted.

"It's okay," he soothed, needing her to know he'd support her in whatever happened and whatever she'd had to do. Because he loved her, and that was all that mattered.

Dove squeezed her tight, inhaled the scent of her, and thanked God for her safe delivery. He'd find out what happened later, but for now, this was enough.

The grief finally melted away, and he didn't quite know what more to say.

"I helped, didn't I, Dove?" Her whisper clawed at his heart.

"Yes, sweetheart. We're safe for now. It's up to Liam to do his part now. He's rounded up the wounded, and they're sending out crews to assist with the disposal of remains."

He knew she was aware of what that meant. She'd told him she'd heard from others that the only effective control was to burn the bodies.

"I don't…"

"Shhh," he whispered against her temple. "I doubt he'd expect your assistance with that. Let's go inside and you can have a drink and something to eat."

He turned her, slowly, and led her into the building, where the food had been prepared by those who'd remained in the main building once the *all clear* had gone out. Basic though the food was, the sandwiches, made with thick hunks of bread, salads, and even some ham would fill hungry bellies and was an initial but immediate thank you.

Dove pulled her into the line, shoved a plate at her, and she moved to the table, taking a couple of items, then moved away as he did the same. They found a spot on a set of old steps and settled. He knew he'd be called upon soon, but she needed him first.

They'd barely taken a bite when a runner came. "Dove, Liam needs you. Says he needs to make arrangements."

He swallowed a snatch, accepted the note the boy handed over, and scanned it.

Another settlement has been attacked. They were prepared thanks to our alert, but things are dire. They've requested assistance from you.
Liam

It wasn't quite what he'd expected. "Where is he?"

"At the ammunition storage unit. He asked if you can come now."

Dove rose and held out a hand to his wife.

Leonie's face betrayed her surprise. "You want me to come with you?"

The nod he gave her was decisive, and she stood and followed him down the stairs, plate still in hand, as the munitions storage wasn't far away.

They turned the corner, and Dove noted the rifles being stored in the large lockers they'd found in a local high school.

"Good, you're here. We have a community, not too far from here. They took casualties and have asked if you'd give them last rites." Liam talked as they counted off the rifles and checked the ammunition.

"I can, but I want a car so Leonie can come with me. The wife of a priest is more than just that. Her role is helper and confidante. Comforter too."

Liam whirled. "That can be arranged. But first, we deal with our own. Tonight at sunset. We'll gather in the refectory. The people will need time to grieve, and you're good at helping them come to terms with losses."

Surprise bloomed at the ease in which his request was granted. Leonie tugged on his sleeve, and he turned. "What about my class?"

Liam sighed. "We're not going to be able to resume normal classes for a few days, so time away is fine."

Leonie shook her head. "No. They need routine and stability," she argued, and while Dove understood that, he had to agree with Liam.

"Right now, parents need to keep their kids close, and just in case there are any more incursions, it makes sense to keep the alert status. Liam's right. I wouldn't resume classes for a couple more days."

She glowered but allowed them to continue the planning. They'd leave first thing in the morning. Jamie and Theodore, another guard, would be their escort on motorbikes, and they'd use the reinforced vehicle Liam had utilized today.

"We're going to round everyone up. Send them to their houses. Give them some time to relax. The disposal duty should be almost finished." All heads turned to the smoke rising in the air at the far end of the compound, where such rituals now routinely took place.

"Do you want me to alert everyone?"

Liam shook his head. "No, Ramon and his crew will do that. Go on home. Take a breather. There's not much that can be done until sunset."

Dove accepted Liam's direction, took Leonie's hand, though she seemed stiff, and together they headed for the tiny shed house he had called home for over a year.

As he held the door, he noted the tension in the set of her shoulders.

"Did I do or say something wrong, Leonie?"

She whirled. "You just jumped in to agree with Liam. I know times are different, but you could have at least listened to me." Tears shone in her eyes.

He opened his mouth, then realized he probably looked like a landed fish, mouth gaping and closing. "I'm sorry. I just meant—"

With a whoosh of air, Leonie deflated into a chair, a woebegone expression on her face. "I'm sorry," she muttered. "You're right. I just…" She shrugged, and he slumped into the seat beside her.

"No. I should have listened, and you're right. But as much as I want to agree with you, these decisions have to be made, and I agreed with Liam. Until the threat has passed, it's better to have the children at home with their parents."

"Yeah." She gazed forward, staring into the distance. "It's hard having someone else to explain everything to, Dove. I'm not used to it."

He pulled her close. "It's okay, Leonie. We're all trying to make the best of the situation."

Snuffling, she laid her head on his shoulder. "I know. I guess I'm just trying to find my feet and sometimes…"

"Come on. Let's have a shower, then you can rest while I get ready."

He didn't expect her to bolt upright. "I'll help you, Dove. That's what I should be doing."

"After the shower," he agreed and watched as she rose and turned to him.

"Come on then. You could maybe wash my back."

Chapter 11

Morning came early, and Leonie dragged herself from the warm covers as Dove did the same. They'd packed a change of clothes, unsure how long they'd be away but aware it would more than likely require an overnight stay.

In the dimness of dawn, they carried the bags and Dove's wooden case to Elaine and Liam's where Jamie and Theodore met them. She'd never met Theodore before and doubted she would have passed more than a few words with him before what they now called the apocalypse. He was burly with tattoos festooning his arms, his dark hair long and tied back with a leather thong, and when he smiled, she caught a flash of metal in his mouth.

"Theodore was a biker before all this," Dove had told her, and she could see that, but she held out her hand and made his acquaintance. After all, they were equal in the face of the zombies, she guessed.

"Nice to meet you," she said, then stashed her bag on the backseat of the vehicle. It looked atrocious. Old and rusted, with plates of iron screwed onto the body. She eyed it, wondering if they'd make it to the community.

"Not to worry, missus. I serviced her myself. Beforehand I was the resident mechanic for our group. No one ever complained," Theodore proudly announced.

I wonder if that was based on his skill or everyone was just plain scared of him! She kept her mouth shut, smiled, and nodded.

Dove clambered in beside her and waited for Jamie's signal to start the vehicle. It hummed to life, and she wondered at the ingenuity of this motley group who'd built a thriving community.

"He's a bit scary when you first meet him, but he has a heart of gold. The biker group he belonged to ran regular deliveries to the hospitals at Christmas and Easter before this happened. He also was a member of the local Big Brother chapter." Dove's voice held a lilt of laughter, and she stared at him.

"Really?"

"Theodore's more than he seems. Lost his mother and wife in the apocalypse, and that really hurt him. He managed to find his daughter a few months later, and she's here, living on the community with him. He's not long remarried, and his wife is pregnant. She was one of the ones in the hospital during the attack yesterday. She's due any day now." Dove guided the vehicle out of the gates as he spoke, and they passed the trip discussing the people they'd met and their stories.

"You know, when this is done, someone should write the story of the community. I mean, what you've told me today…well, it's amazing. Doctors and nurses, a rubbish man, and a chef," she marveled aloud.

"Yes, but the strangest thing of all is many have found their soul mates here. It's like some great hand was guiding them to be here at the right time to meet the other who completes them. Like when I found you, Leonie."

His words, softly spoken, filled her with a flush of pleasure. "I think you might be onto something there."

They finished the drive in silence, and it was only when they saw the plume of smoke on the horizon they spoke again. "We're not far away, are we?" she asked.

Dove peered at the smoke. "No." He pulled the car to a halt at Jamie's signal and wound down the window.

"I'm going ahead," said Jamie. "Theodore will wait with you, and you know the routine. Anything odd, you get moving. I'll be back as quickly as I can."

Dove appeared unconcerned as Jamie climbed from his bike and pushed it into the shade while Theodore took up position on Dove's side. Leonie hated the waiting, in case the situation wasn't as they'd been led to expect.

Nerves jittered until the sound of Jamie returning settled her a little.

He pulled off his helmet, and his shoulders slumped. "It's all good ahead, but they had a rough time. Lost quite a few of their community, so they're going to need you. They're working hard to reinstate their defenses, but they have a long way to go."

Once his helmet was back in place, they followed Jamie forward, the settlement coming into view. The destruction was phenomenal. Fencing hung at crazy angles, buildings with smashed doors and windows. Chunks of wood littered the street of what had once been a tidy though small town, and she scanned it all as they passed.

Some walls were spattered with dark blood, and bile rose in Leonie's throat. "So much destruction."

They stopped the car and climbed out by the old hall in the center of the township. A woman, maybe in her fifties, stepped forward. "Dove, it's so good to see you." Her salt-and-pepper hair straggled down her back, the bun she'd contained it in clearly having failed some time back.

"Karen, you know Jamie and Theodore, and this is my wife, Leonie."

The woman's eyes lit with wonder. "Well now, that's lovely to hear, but I didn't know…"

Leonie stepped forward. "It's lovely to meet you. Looks like you have a nice community here."

Karen's face dropped into a frown. "We weren't prepared. We got the message from Liam, but…" She shrugged. "I guess we thought we were safe. Far enough out of town to not present any issue. I was wrong, and my mistake cost us all."

Dove placed a gentle hand on Karen's. "He was contacting

everyone quickly, and maybe we didn't explain the severity of the situation."

"No, Dove. Complacency is never a good thing. I know Liam wants to talk about a strike team, and I've spoken with our remaining community directors. They won't accept my resignation and have agreed to talks with Liam. We shouldn't have to live in fear. Something has to happen." Karen pushed up the sleeves of her shirt as they entered an old, rickety hall. "Well, if you set up in here, I'll have everyone gathered later today. Shouldn't take long to get the gates and fences back in place. I have a list of our losses here." She thrust a sheet of paper at him.

Leonie noted the length of the list. In brackets beside each was a number she assumed to be ages. Their losses included infants, and an ache started in her breast.

"Do you need some help? I can make food, clean houses. Just name it and I'm there."

Karen smiled, a tired and tight effort in Leonie's estimation. "No, dear. You stay here. Assist your husband. We've got this." Then Karen strode away.

Dove's hand captured hers. "That was kind. They're proud in this community. They mostly weathered the initial attacks with few losses and worked to fortify what they had. Karen used to be mayor, and the people asked her to remain in the position of authority. She's taken this hard." His eyes followed the retreating back of the woman. "They'll be okay eventually. It's just a lot to lose, and many of them children."

They worked hard, cleaning the hall out and setting it up, including chairs. Karen came back and Dove asked if they had photos of those they lost. The woman scrubbed a shaking hand over her face. "I'll see what we can find." Then she hurried back out.

At the front of the room, he set up a temporary altar, and for the first time, Leonie got a look at the contents of his box. It brought back memories of before the attacks. She knew he'd celebrated services when she'd been simply staying with him, but she'd stayed away. Now, Leonie realized just how such a celebration of life had bolstered her as she'd grown up.

"I missed this," she murmured, and he turned with a smile on his face.

"Us?" He kept the word light and flirtatious, as if he realized the shock the realization came with.

"No, silly. This. Belief." She waved her hand around the room. "I didn't attend before when you had services because I didn't want to remember. There were such good times when I grew up. When times got tough the church was there, you know? The priest didn't expect us to go every week, and I think that's the secret. When we needed him he was there. Father Jerome was a pretty cluey man and understood that we as teens needed to feel we had choices. He never turned us away when we needed a shoulder or ear though."

Dove waited, as if knowing she needed to say the words.

"I never really had the time to thank him once the apocalypse happened. He was the first in town to pass. Had a heart attack saying mass after we heard."

Now Leonie stopped and breathed fast, trying to hold off her sense of loss. Tears dripped down her face, and the grief just leached out of her.

"I'm not a wimp, Dove. I don't melt into a puddle when things go wrong, but I can't seem to stop myself from crying." This lack of control infuriated her, and she clenched her fists, willing the horrible emotions away.

He enfolded her in his arms. "It's okay to feel grief, Leonie. Times are hard, but we can and should allow our bodies to show the physical signs of that. On a physical level, it releases endorphins to help lift our spirits. Emotionally, it lets us feel like our bodies are washing away the bad stuff."

"Well, the endorphins are picking a really bad time to show themselves," she muttered, and he laughed.

"Karen's organized a quick meal for us before we begin." Slinging an arm around her shoulder, he urged her to the front of the building and down the steps. They'd barely exited when a growl split the air.

Adrenaline coursed.

Her brain demanded action.

Leonie turned, noting the zombie lurching toward them, and she pushed Dove back, heard him stumble and fall. She cursed, willing him to rise.

"Run!" Leonie's scream echoed loud as the rotting creature reached for her.

She spun, hearing the sounds of feet pounding near her.

The green-gray flesh of the hand of the monster reached again, swiping, and the fetid breath washed over her face. Stomach churning, she dodged, then tripped.

This is it. All over. Squeezing her eyes shut so she wouldn't see it looming, Leonie huddled on the ground, hands clutched over her head.

A crack echoed, and she looked up in time to see the zombie waver. The bright red shine of the eyes dimmed before the zombie slumped to the ground, a spatter of wet liquid covering her.

"Leonie." Dove was there, reaching down, and she rose, her body trembling.

"Oh, Dove!" It was all she could manage as he held her close. "I've never been so afraid," she whimpered, and she felt the twin pounding of his heart and hers.

"Damn it. It must have been hiding out the day," Karen snarled behind her as she lowered the rifle. "Are you all okay?"

As if realizing he hadn't checked, Dove released her and began almost manically patting her down. "Blood. Whose blood?"

"His. Its. The zombie's." Her brain struggled to find a normal plateau, and merely answering the question nearly undid her.

"You need a wash, Leonie. Come on and follow me." Leonie and Dove turned at Karen's words. "Hmm, you both do, it seems. I'll get someone to clear up here before we begin."

They trailed Karen, Dove holding Leonie close as if unable to release her, and she not only welcomed but needed that support.

They entered a small house nearby. "The bathroom is through there. This is where you'd be staying tonight anyway, so take your time. We have water, though it's rationed. Dove can fill you in."

She left, and they stood there eyeing each other. "My clothes," Leonie whispered.

Dove nodded. "I'll get Jamie and Theodore to bring them in. Bathroom's through here. Run some water into the sink, and I'll join you in a minute."

He pushed her through a door, and she noted an old-fashioned tub, a small sink, and towels, then sighed.

Water flowed from the faucet, warm from the sun, she guessed, and a bar of soap—one of the small guest ones you'd find in a motel room—sat in front of her.

With a quick glance at the door she'd closed behind her, Leonie stripped off her shirt, wadded it up, and threw it into the corner. "Never wearing that one again."

Two raps told her Dove had returned, and she stepped back, gripped the door, and let him in. In his hand were their bags.

His gaze settled on her. She knew what he saw. The smears of blood which had seeped through her shirt and the same in her hair.

"Let's get you cleaned up." Dove picked up the face washer and set to work.

* * *

NIGHT HAD FALLEN and they were finally alone in the small room of the traveler's house Karen had set aside for Dove's use. The bed was big enough for the two, though it was a little snug.

He kept his arm around Leonie and waited for sleep to come, more than expecting a nightmare for her.

They'd come so close to losing each other with the zombie having waited until they'd emerged to attack. Even now, the memory left him chilled.

When that hand reached for Leonie he'd risen, mind disengaged as he'd lifted a rock from beside the stairs, ready to take that life. Was it right? His brain told him the zombie was no longer a human and would kill his wife. His soul, on the other hand, felt stained and shredded by the knowledge he would have done that.

Karen's swift action had saved him from that reality.

Even now, his fingers clenched, and his body tensed in memory.

"Dove?" Leonie's voice was muffled by the pillow, but he heard it clear enough.

"What's wrong?" He leaned over, needing to ensure she was as comfortable as he could make her.

"It's okay, you know. I know you were afraid. I was too. Terrified you'd be dead and…" Leonie sat up in the bed, and he moved back, letting her settle herself against the pillows. "I love you, and the thought that anything might happen to you just tears me apart. Dove, you're the most important person in my life."

He waited as she struggled with her emotions.

"I don't want to lose you." Humbled, he rubbed his eyes and pinched the bridge of his nose. "I picked up a rock. I was willing to do whatever I could to protect you, Leonie. I'm not a violent man, but in that moment…"

Leonie's eyes widened, and her mouth formed an 'o' of surprise. "Wow. I didn't know… That's…" She shook her head.

"I know. But I'd protect you." There didn't seem to be much else to say.

She scooted over closer and rested her head on his shoulder, as if reassuring both of them of their current status.

"When we return to the community, I need to see Liam. Let him know they hide. In case we missed one at home."

She gasped. "I didn't…"

"I'm sure Karen radioed it in, but I need to tell him face-to-face. We need to share the news, so others can be on the lookout. He needs to bring forward his plans to work with the others, because if he doesn't…" The words stuck in his throat.

"They're advancing rapidly. If we don't control the situation now, then we may not be able to." She finished the thought he couldn't get out.

"Yes."

Time passed in silence. "Dove? Will you make love to me? Here and now?" She turned in his arms and pressed her mouth against his.

He moved, settling down lower in the bed and pulling her with him. He slid his mouth away from hers. "I wasn't going to ask because I wasn't sure you'd—"

"Shut up and kiss me back," she breathed against the flesh of his lips.

He did, running his hands up and down her form and letting his worries melt away.

Her hands moved, sliding their way under the light t-shirt he wore, and found his nipples. Her fingers rounded the jutting flesh, and he groaned. His body flamed, and he tugged her closer so she lay over him, and he captured her ankles with his feet so their bodies nestled together.

When his cock, jutting through his boxers, nudged against her belly, she gasped, pulling upward, and her breasts thrust forward.

"So beautiful," he muttered and spun them in the bed so she now was beneath him. "Hidden treasures for me."

"That may be so, but I want you naked, Dove. I want to feel you moving inside me. I want to feel the burn of passion and the ecstasy. I want to share it with you and you only."

He leaned away and slipped his hands down to her panties, the elastic granting him access, and for a moment, he palmed the rounded swell of her ass before sliding the material down her legs. His gaze settled on the tiny thatch of hair that covered her, his body hot, and his skin prickled. *Mine. My woman.* The primitive thoughts pounded through him, blood rushing in his veins.

"Like what you see?"

In the dimness he caught sight of the eagerness on her face, the slight swelling of her lips from his kisses, and the rosy flush of arousal. Her nipples jutted against the tank top she wore for a night-shirt, and he reached up, touching the nub through the cotton. Her eyes shut and she moaned, squirmed beneath his touch, and the spike that slid through his senses urged him to do more. Show her more.

With careful, though shaking fingers, he captured the hem of the top and slipped it up, noting that it caught momentarily against the swell of her breasts. Leonie sat up and slid the shirt over her head.

"Your turn," she said.

He grinned and stripped down. Once more he had her naked and willing before him. With his mouth, he found the sensitive flesh at the side of her neck and nuzzled, licked, and kissed while his hands slid over her, reacquainting themselves with her body.

Leonie's fingers dug deep, her nails biting into the skin and sinews at his shoulders, but he didn't care because they were together in the moment.

Moving down her body, he worshipped one breast then the other, delighting in flicking at her nipples with his tongue. They responded by stiffening, and her gasps of pleasure had his body tightening further. With a final lick, he moved lower, dipping his tongue into her navel after circling it.

Hunger urged him to part her legs and inhale her scent. *Musky.*

He settled his mouth over her and feasted. Leonie squirmed and clenched through his ministrations, her wetness and divine taste driving him insane.

Dove felt the moment her orgasm shot as she stiffened and cried out.

More. He'd give her more and himself. But for a moment he tasted her essence as her body settled against him.

Pulling away, he reared back and watched his wife relax. Saw the rapid pounding of her pulse, the jump of the vein in her neck slow as she came down from the high. The need burning in his veins turned incandescent, and he moved, crawling up her body.

"I'm not done yet," he whispered, and her eyes flashed open.

"Really?"

The curve of her lips as she smiled urged him forward. He kissed her, knowing she'd taste herself on his mouth.

Tongues tangled, and he pulled her into position, then he captured her breasts, sliding his fingers over the engorged nipples as she reached down, cupping him.

He pulled away with a groan, his mind splintering. "If you…do that, we won't…" The words emerged on gasps as his body demanded satisfaction

Leonie captured his mouth, cutting off the words, and wrapped her legs around his waist.

He plunged when his cock felt the warm, heated glove he craved. He slid deep then held still as her body once more pulsed and throbbed, milking him.

Unable to stop himself, he started moving, wild hammering urging his own orgasm. His hips thrust back and forth, and her thighs gripped him tight. She cried out again, throwing her head back as he came, shooting the hot semen deep into her body.

Holding her still, he waited for the wild throb of his heart to slow. Thinking was like pushing his way through molasses. The only knowledge was that he loved her. That the emotions consuming him were shared by her.

Slumping down, Dove took her with him, so she cuddled against him, soft and pliant in the aftermath of their lovemaking.

"Well now, that was *hawt*," Leonie said, and she laughed at her own words.

He laughed too. "It was. But we should sleep now, because tomorrow will be busy." Dove settled his wife against him, his hand resting between her breasts so he could feel the steadied beat of her heart. "Sleep well, my love."

THE ZOMBIE ADVANCED, its claws long and its teeth open, ready to bite. It would be on her in a moment, and all she could do was curl into a ball. Its breath, hot and stinking, enveloped her in its ripe scent, and she opened her mouth to scream. Thin and long, it erupted.

"Wake up." Dove's hand urged Leonie to awareness.

Opening her eyes, she was met with darkness and the solid heat of Dove's body against hers. Her chest bellowed and her skin felt cold and clammy. "Dove?"

"It's okay. You're safe now."

"Where… Where are we?" She shivered, and he pulled the bedclothes closer around their nude bodies.

"Safe. Inside, and nothing can get to us." His words reassured, but they weren't in their home and…

It took all her concentration to push aside the bubble of terror that still clawed at her insides. "We aren't at home," she offered, well aware the words sounded lame.

"No. We're going home today."

She relaxed a little more, releasing the now tensed muscles. "Today? It's morning?"

"Almost." Dove sighed. "The zombie attack yesterday triggered your nightmare."

She nodded and picked at the bedsheet. For some reason this attack triggered her enough to cause the dream she hadn't faced after the attack on the community. Her mind helpfully offered the insight that it was because she'd known Dove was in danger and she hadn't been able to do anything about it except curl up in a fetal ball.

The knowledge scoured her. "I froze. Right there on the damned grass."

"You were in danger and your body took over. It happens."

Tears burned her eyes. "But if I'd done more—"

"You would likely have died. Then I'd have to cope with that forever. Don't do this, Leonie. Beating yourself to a pulp because of *may have's* doesn't help anyone."

"Maybe," she muttered as she rose from the bed.

Leonie felt the heat of his gaze watching as she hunted for clothes and dressed. Anger scorched her, and though her brain told her it was silly to be furious at both of them, she was.

He climbed out, met her at the side of the bed, and slipped his arms around her. "Why are you so angry? It doesn't make sense."

"I don't know," she wailed, dropping her head to his shoulder. "I know what you've said, but it doesn't make it easier. When will this…" She waved her hand in the direction of 'out there'. "…get better?"

"I don't know. All I can say is if we let it beat us down, we'll drown in regrets and fear. We're survivors, my love. We have to hold onto that knowledge."

She slumped down on the bed. "I know you're right." She sniffled. "I just feel like I have so much and there are lots who have less. Surely I should be able to do more with what I have?"

"We do what we can. We appreciate those who do what we can't, and we actively practice thankfulness." His intent in his words filled her thoughts.

Thankfulness. "It sucks when you come out with the wise bullshit, Dove. But you're right, and I know it in here." Leonie tapped her head, well aware she sounded sulky.

He grinned. "I know, but you love me anyway."

Chapter 12

Dove waited impatiently outside Liam and Elaine's house. They had arrived back at camp only a short time before, but the revelation about the zombies was too important to leave until later.

The door opened and Ramon stalked out, followed by one of the scientists who'd since made her home at the community. "Ramon, wait!" She scurried after him, rolling her eyes while Liam's brother retreated.

Liam appeared at the door. "Sorry to keep you waiting, Dove, but Ramon had an issue that needed to be dealt with sensitively."

A brief moment of wondering what it could be passed, and he trailed Liam through the door. "Sorry, but while I'm sure Karen apprised you of the attack—"

"No. What attack?" He seemed genuinely surprised, so Dove dropped into the seat and waited as Liam did the same. "Tell me about it."

"We were at their compound, had finished setting up for the memorial session when we went outside. We were…" He fished for an appropriate term. "…accosted by a zombie, but no one was hurt."

Liam frowned. "No one saw the creature?"

Dove shook his head. "They're starting to *think*, Liam. It had to have hidden because they'd almost finished erecting the fences and gates. They would have seen it."

His friend turned ashen. "That's bad."

"What's bad?" queried Elaine as she entered the room.

"Zombies. Thinking." Liam winced even as he repeated what Dove had suggested.

"Yeah. We need to get the word out now. Have to start making those alliances, because if we don't…" Dove didn't finish the sentence, because he could see Liam coming to the same conclusion.

Liam rose, paced with jerky movements to one end of the room, then back. "Ramon says the one we caught was capable of rudimentary communication. This is downright scary stuff. We need help. Outside help."

"We do, but where do we go from here?"

"We talk to Camp Queanbeyan first. Julia's stepfather has connections, and we need to raise an army against the militia."

"But the people here aren't trained army, Liam. The militia have access to munitions we don't. There's no way we can beat them." Dove's stomach curdled.

"True, but we have you."

Dove blinked. "Pardon?"

"We need someone to go inside. To see what their setup is. We know a few members of the camp managed to get away from the militia, but they don't last long. None of the communities are willing to open their doors to them. But a priest? He might just be able to—"

"No." Dove shook his head. "I can't."

Liam stared at him. "If you don't, I can't see any way that we can find out. Look for their weaknesses, Dove. We need assistance, but how do we tell them what's there if we can't—"

Elaine cleared her throat. "There were actually groups of priests way back to Tudor times who assisted with espionage. I remember reading about it before everything happened. We need you, Dove. We need what you represent."

Heat scorched his face. "I can't."

"Think about it. Talk to Leonie, but consider that this could save those of us who are still alive. We need every bit of help we can get. Please." Liam's entreaty fed the sourness that settled on his tongue.

"I have to go."

Leaving the building with rapid steps, Dove tried to banish the knowledge of what Liam had requested from him. It felt like a betrayal of everything he was.

It's a slippery slope once you choose to bend your morals. But by the same token, he could save lives.

Would he be able to look himself in the eye if he complied? How could he not do his part? The arguments ran around his mind, and every counterargument was like being hit over the head, which now ached.

He let himself into the house and headed for the fridge.

Leonie emerged from their bedroom, a smile on her face. It faded as she looked at him. "Dove?" Her feet tapped quickly over the floor as she neared him. "Tell me."

"Liam asked me to…" He felt nauseous simply saying what had been asked. "…to spy on the militia. They've asked me to go in as a priest, gather as much information as I can, and relay it back."

"What?" She rocked back on her heels. "How could he ask that of you?"

He laid a hand on her shoulder. "There are arguments for and against it. I just don't know what I should do. If I do it, I could save lives. Lots of them. Ramon says the zombies now have rudimentary communication abilites, and Liam and I agree this means—"

"They're evolving. Holy mother of God." Her hand flattened on her belly.

"Exactly. Liam's asked me to think about it, and I don't know what to do, Leonie. I could ignore it and continue on. That's the easy path, but I feel it's the wrong one. I could do what he asks and collect information, but that's against my belief system. But if I did, we might have a fighting chance. Elaine said priests have been spies for centuries, but right now, that doesn't make me feel better about my options, or lack of them." He speared his fingers through his hair.

Leonie watched him, her concern clear. "I can't tell you what to do, Dove. Only you can make that decision." She slid tender arms around his waist. "But whatever you decide to do, I will support you."

Closing his eyes, he absorbed her strength.

Chapter 13

Leonie watched the frown form on her husband's face. He'd told her of leaving Camp Queanbeyan as they'd termed the old hospital. He'd never intended to return, yet here they were, in the small car with Liam, Elaine, and baby Isla. Motorcycles flanked them, Jamie and Theodore among the four.

She wondered how Dove viewed the building as it loomed before them. Large, wrought iron gates blocked out the unwelcome zombies. The trip had been frighteningly uneventful, and for the first time, Leonie wondered where all the other zombies were.

The description of his travel on the bus, how the zombies had dropped from the bridge, had her terrified they'd accost the outriders, yet it remained calm.

"I haven't seen one," Liam muttered, and Leonie glanced at Dove, who was driving the vehicle as Liam and Elaine filled the backseat with their musings.

"No. Liam, have there been less sightings in the last few weeks?" Dove glanced into the mirror, and she wondered what he was looking at.

"Now that you say that, yeah. Strangely, there have been very few sightings."

Leonie twisted in her seat. "What about these militia sightings? You said they'd been rounding the zombies up, right? What if they've got what's left?"

Dove grunted. "If they have, then the problem is much bigger than we anticipated."

"I doubt you'll get a look at the pens, Dove. Leonie, maybe you could carefully ask around. Someone might have something to say about those holding pens and how many are in them. But remember, you have to take care with your questioning. They're going to be on guard, and one slip will endanger your mission," Elaine reminded her.

"I'm not taking my wife in there," Dove growled.

Leonie laid her hand on his. "I can go. I'll be able to help."

He vibrated beneath her touch. "No."

She glared at him. "Yes. You need me, and I'm not staying behind without you. And no matter what you say, I'll follow by myself if you leave me behind."

His lips thinned. "No."

"Yes." And this time she nodded, comfortable that she would indeed do so.

He stopped talking and gave his full attention back to the drive as if letting his mind consider her demands as he drove.

Today, they were heading to the old hospital to attend a meeting. The commandant—a horrible man, according to Dove—wanted to make sure they were capable. And Liam felt, as the biggest military style community, that having them on side would be an asset.

The gates opened ahead of them, and they entered. Dove eased the car up the overgrown driveway which still bore the title of *Emergency Department*.

The car glided to a stop, but Dove kept it idling, and Leonie slid her white-knuckled hand over one of his. "We'll be in and out in no time."

He grunted, turned off the car, and pocketed the keys. As they climbed out of the car, she looked down the drive, noting the now closed gates and guards in military fatigues, rifles in hand, flanking them.

They hung back as Elaine and Liam carried the baby into the building, and Leonie held Dove's hand. "It'll be okay, Dove. He can't say anything or make you do anything you don't want to. You can leave the meeting at any time, and I'll be waiting for you."

They stepped inside, and the scent of bodies, some unwashed, hit like a tangible force.

"Oh my gosh." She slid her hand over her face and looked at Elaine who showed distaste at the stench.

"We'll head for the cafeteria and meet you guys there." Elaine ushered Leonie to the room where she could smell food cooking.

The room was clean but showed the signs of lack of care and over-use. Tables were scarred and the seats sagging. They grabbed chairs nestled against the wall and slid them around a vacant table.

A woman sidled up. "You want coffee, you get your own. It's over there." She pointed to a large urn and a pile of tins. A tub with cups sat beside it.

Leonie wondered about the health and well-being of some of the clientele, and there was enough concern to steer her away from both beverages and food.

"Which community are you from?" The woman who'd addressed them slouched against the edge of the table.

"Uh, the Big Farm Community," Elaine answered, giving the woman the name the inhabitants had agreed on.

The woman's eyes lit up. "You know J?"

Leonie frowned, but Elaine nodded. "Sure, Julia. Yeah, she's an important member of our community."

"She was here before she met that Leroy. Left with him and Dove in tow when things got bad for her, and I couldn't blame her a bit. Miss that priest a lot though. He'd offer lots of worthwhile advice, and people took comfort in his words. Oh, and he was easy on the eyes." The woman grinned, then it melted away under the weight of memories, by the looks of it. "Only thing is the commandant didn't take to him. He wasn't gun happy like most of the inhabitants, so old Commie didn't see a use for him."

Leonie's eyes had widened at the woman's comments about Dove, but it was the description of the commandant's view of him that had her blood boiling. "Dove's an important person. He's the pastoral carer and—"

"Hang on. I get that. He was here too. I think Commie was struggling at the time with the problems of command. Anyway, you tell J that Casey says hi, okay?"

The woman retreated, and for a moment, Leonie let anxiety fill her at the thought that she'd scared the woman off. *If that was all it took…well, I can't help that.*

The baby, Isla, started to fuss, and Elaine looked to her. "I gotta feed her." She fumbled with her shirt and laid the baby against her breast.

Leonie wondered how it would feel to grow a child, feed it, and share the future with a tiny human being who was not just totally physically reliant on you, but also dependent on you to help it grow into a good person. How would Dove react if she were pregnant?

Not the right time. Soon. When things settle.

The idea took root though, and she realized how often their intimacies took place without protection. She bit her lip and wondered if she could already be expecting.

DOVE REFUSED to allow the blustering man to upset him. He'd been in this position before, heard all the posturing. For the first time, it meant very little to him.

"—he's not capable of this kind of intelligence gathering. He *ran away* when things got tough before, and now you expect me to—"

Liam shot out of his chair, while Dove sat still, little more than an onlooker. "I will not tolerate your negativity toward my people. You can run Camp Queanbeyan however you like, but Dove is one of mine now. He's earned the respect of the community." Liam's face flushed, and Dove was intrigued by the passionate defense the man put up.

The commandant subsided under the correction of Liam, and for the first time, Dove could see the man was full of hot air and self-absorption.

Liam indicated that Dove should say his piece, so he straightened up in the chair and looked the aging man in the face. "I'm more than able to undertake this mission, but this isn't the first. The reason Liam wants your agreement is simply because we believe that gaining intelligence will allow us to tailor our defenses against the militia. Without that," Dove said, shrugging, "we're fighting shadows. We need to know how many of the mutated zombies they've got. We believe that they've cleared most from this area and are massing them to complete the initial task Allan Anterrum warned about last year. That a facet of the government has been building an army and plan a coup. That cannot be allowed, because even this facility will not withstand them."

The man stared at Dove, his jaw open. "You cannot be serious."

"We've never been more so, commandant," answered Liam. "Call Anterrum and he'll tell you exactly what I've said. During his last visit to the community we held discussions about just this matter. We both agree that something has to happen."

"But *him?*" The derision in the commandant's words would once have cut Dove like a knife through butter, but not anymore. And Dove realized in the time since he'd left here, he'd not just grown into what he could be, but also now valued himself for what he was capable of.

"I'm more than able, and your bully tactics don't work on me anymore, commandant." Dove rose and headed for the door, but before he left, he turned to deliver a final salvo. "Good leaders build up their people. Poor leaders tear them down. Excellent leaders know when it's time to change their ways."

Stepping beyond the door, Dove inhaled deeply and noted the many faces of those waiting outside. Some he knew, but many he didn't. He inclined his head toward them all and retreated to the cafeteria, realizing that's where the two women would likely wait for both himself and Liam.

He had nothing more to offer to the meeting, and he and Liam had both agreed that when his part was done, he should leave and allow Liam to lay out the plan.

Striding down the corridor, he felt as if he had a use in this new look society.

The entrance to the cafeteria was emblazoned in red and white, but he felt no affinity with the place. It was as if a different person had lived here for a year or more and participated in missions. But that person was no longer him.

How odd was that, he mused, then he smiled. "It feels good too."

LEONIE WRAPPED her hands around the cup. She and Elaine had been here some time, and they knew it looked totally obvious that they had nothing before them, so they'd agreed to get tea. Hold the mugs until the men returned. It didn't take long, and when Dove returned, she gratefully slid the cup onto the table and stepped up to him.

His arms folded around her, and the kiss they shared could have melted the vinyl on the use-darkened seats.

The woman called Casey came bustling over, took one look at the two of them, and her jaw dropped open. "Dove. You… You kissed her?"

Dove glanced at Leonie, and she grinned up at him.

"Sure, this is my wife, Leonie." His words soothed the ragged edges of concern she'd carried for him. From what little Julia and Leroy had said of Camp Queanbeyan, she'd actually expected hostility from pretty much everyone here. Clearly that wasn't quite accurate.

"Well, color me surprised. I thought you'd settled for celibacy and just do your priestly stuff." The woman rested against the edge of the seat, hand on hip. "I have to be honest, I never expected this."

Holding Leonie close against his side, he answered with something that sounded suspiciously like, "me either," but she was far too distracted to give the words her full attention. Instead she was interested by the arrival of what she would term a 'very important man' from his swagger, as he headed in their direction.

She nudged Dove with an elbow to the ribs, and both he and Elaine stiffened.

"Good to see you both here. I guess Liam is too?" The man's voice was carefully modulated, and he carried an air of self-possession about him.

Dove straightened up. "Yes, he is, Mr. Anterrum. He'll be along here shortly."

The man smiled, though Leonie noted it didn't meet his eyes. "Good. I'm actually planning on traveling back later today. Don't suppose you have space?"

Leonie watched the by-play, wondering who the man was and why he was trying to catch a ride back to the community with them. She'd never seen him before, though to be fair, she'd only been there just over a month and was still coming to know those who considered themselves community members.

"Sadly, not this time. I'm sure the commandant will be able to find a ride for you though, and I'd think you could travel in convoy with us."

The man's mouth tightened. "And do you plan to introduce me to these lovely ladies and…" Mr. Anterrum's voice died away.

"I thought you remembered Elaine, Liam's wife, and their daughter, Isla. This is my wife, Leonie," he answered, and unease coursed through her.

What's the deal, she wanted to ask, but she restrained the question until later. If she'd learned nothing else during this time, it was that sometimes keeping it in your head was the wisest action.

"Lovely to meet you." Anterrum shook her hand, and she had the distinct urge to wash the oil from it when he was done.

The man uttered a platitude, informed them he'd see them later, and drifted away.

"Who was that?" enquired Leonie.

Elaine leaned forward with a conspiratorial wink and answered, "He's Julia's stepfather, and he used to be some kind of bigwig in the government before it all went sour. Now he's involved in trying to get things sorted out."

It didn't really explain much as far as she could tell, so Leonie determined to ask Dove what that meant later on. "He's coming to the community?"

Dove watched the man making his way through the throngs in the cafeteria, and Leonie observed the emotions rolling across his face, muscles jerking and the planes of his cheeks tightening then releasing. "Seems like. I wonder if he's also going to run for head of state once we regain control of the country?"

The comment startled Leonie. "*What?* You think he's looking to use this?" If he was, well, to her way of thinking that was just plain…*sick*. Surely no one would. The idea felt like it melted her brain.

Dove eyed her. "It's why we're in this mess. Someone had a great idea and wanted to use it to increase their popularity with the voters. When it all went wrong, it was a case of who to blame in the media. The people remember these things, the same as they remember those who want to put things to rights again."

Leonie huffed out a breath as a wave of nausea threatened to swamp her. To hear them discussing what happened in such a cold and bloodless manner… It shocked her.

Dove cupped her face, and she leaned in, needing the touch. "Maybe I'm just a small-town girl, but I can't see how this could be considered great for the populace."

"I didn't say it was," he answered, gazing deeply into her eyes. "I do wish they'd thought it through before they took the actions, causing millions of deaths. But I'm also incredibly grateful on another level, because it brought us together."

She leaned in, felt that jump of nerves and the invisible wire between them drawing her closer. He was going to kiss her, and how she needed that right now.

The sound of footsteps and someone clearing their throat pushed them apart. Liam appeared over Dove's shoulder and grinned. "Well, I would say get a room, but how about we go home instead?"

Leonie's face flamed with embarrassment. They might be newlyweds, but still, she supposed they should show some kind of decorum. When she glanced at Dove, she noted the mirth, which he quickly followed up with a quiet chuckle. She elbowed him in the ribs, but his *oomph* didn't make up for the flaming of her face.

Elaine pushed out of her seat, and Leonie grabbed the baby bag as her friend hefted the sleeping baby in her arms. "I'm ready for home, and so is Isla."

They trooped to the front door, but as they left, Leonie couldn't stop herself from looking back. From inside the doors of the old hospital, she noted the peering face of the commandant, a study of stern lines and unfriendliness.

Chapter 14

"I'm coming with you." Leonie's voice raised again. The same argument they'd had for the past three days raising its ugly head.

"No." Dove stuffed a spare set of clothes into the bag, knowing they'd have to travel light to the outlying communities, and her face set mulishly.

"Why are you being such a bonehead over this? I won't hold you up. I just need to—"

He raised a hand to stop her words. "No. I can't take you. We're going on the bikes. I can't carry you all the way. The fuel situation is precarious, and I'd have to find fuel to refill with an extra person. There's only four of us going this time. Liam, Jamie, Theodore, and myself. We need to move quickly and stay under the radar. Besides, I need you here to go over what we know. The other community leaders are due to arrive tomorrow, and I need you to keep an eye on what's happening here. Elaine's leading the meetings, and we need to split our time effectively."

It wasn't that he didn't want her with him, but things were tense right now. People were on edge and wondering what Liam and Elaine hadn't disclosed—though they'd shared everything they could with the residents. He and Liam had to meet with the few community leaders who'd refused to participate, and Elaine would be dealing with the higher-ups.

He turned and took Leonie in his arms. "Look, I know you're concerned, but to be honest, if we have any hope of keeping the lid on right now, I need you here soothing those who think we've lied. The attack of the zombies has caused havoc among the camp, and it's getting tricky. We've had more arguments in the last week than we've seen in the time I've been here. *Please.* I need you here peacekeeping and keeping everything on track."

Leonie's face paled, and she turned away. "I… I'm scared when you go away. I know when you're on your rounds…where you'll be, but this is different."

The sound of the break in her voice as she spoke speared him with regret. If only his task was as simple as making rounds and offering pastoral care!

"I'm sorry." He gathered her close. "We've barely had time to stop since we got married. I can't promise things will improve soon, because I don't know. The only promise I can make is that I'll always return to you if I'm able."

A sob erupted, and he waited. "But what if you don't?"

The cause of her fears rose and swamped them both. Lies were pretty but destructive, and he refused to pepper their marriage with them. They could all die. Zombies might attack or marauding bands of rebels who attacked unwary travelers strike them down to steal their bikes and the food they carried. The militia could descend before they were prepared. Too many things could go wrong.

Her fingers gripped tight at his waist, but he drew away when the worst of her crying jag had passed. "Leonie, if I die, your life will go on." He captured her gaze with his own, willing her to not just understand, but to accept this was how it had to be. "You'll grieve and hurt and miss me, but I'll rest knowing you're safe here. Please don't ask me for something I can't and won't do. I need you safe so I can do my job and try to save us all."

Her nod was jerky. If only he knew her tells, because deep down he half-expected her to do something to keep him here or to insist on going with him. Or maybe he was wrong and he just wasn't reading her right. Frustration clawed. They really didn't know each other enough to be able to understand and guess, and they might not yet have a chance to build on what they'd already built together.

She moved away, rubbing at her face with shaking hands. "I know." Her eyes shone with moisture as she nodded. "I'm sorry. I shouldn't make this harder on you." Her voice husked as she spoke. "But I just found you, and I'm supposed to let you go and hope you'll come back, and I feel…" Leonie's hands slid into the air, betraying her confusion. "I don't know, at sea. Lost. Here is home now, but that's because you're here."

He sighed. "I understand that. But I have to…" Dove indicated to the backpack laying open on the bed.

She picked up the towel she'd dropped on the floor and handed it to him after smoothing out the creases marring the folds. "I shouldn't do this to you."

He grunted at the lightning change of mood. He'd have to talk to Liam about it, because it left him wondering if this was a female thing. He had such little experience with women. Yes, he'd had a girlfriend at school, but since then, he'd never allowed a woman close to him, and certainly not close enough to understand mood swings.

Swinging the bag onto his back, he straightened and cupped her face. "I'll be back as soon as I can."

She nodded, and he felt the quiver of her nerves, just below the surface of her skin, and he rubbed his thumb over her mouth.

"I love you," he whispered and leaned in for one last, chaste kiss. Lips met and clung, and he dragged himself away before the flare of hunger enveloped him.

He strode out of the room, his mind struggling to overcome the truth that he had to go. Had to leave. If he didn't go now, he wouldn't go at all, and he had a task.

Striding out of the house, he headed for the area where they garaged the bikes and cars. Liam, Theodore, and Jamie waited for him, their gazes pensive.

Without a word, Dove climbed onto the back of the bike he

regularly rode. He knew the speed and the feel. Could almost navigate by braille.

"Trouble?" Liam asked as he reached for his helmet.

Their gazes met. "She's upset."

Liam nodded. "So is Elaine, though with her I'd say it's hormonal, and baby overload isn't helping."

The men climbed onto their bikes and donned helmets. With a savage gesture, Dove started the engine. Hormones he could understand. Baby overload…well, they weren't there yet.

They steered out through the gates and onto the degraded asphalt. The bikes ate up the miles, keeping together with the guards taking front and rear positions.

At some point in the distance, Dove noted smoke and glanced to the side of the road, seeing the plume rising. It wasn't on their route, so they kept going, but he wondered, all the same, who'd lit it.

The sun beat down, hot and burning as they entered the first community. They slid off their bikes. By agreement Theodore remained with them by the front house where the leader lived. Jamie trailed the two men inside.

"Cade?" Dove said, and the man nodded.

"We're from—"

"You're wasting your time. We aren't interested in a war. The militia leave us alone, and we haven't seen any zombies that are different. Leave now."

Liam attempted to explain, but it was like talking to a hammer; blunt and hard striking. After a fruitless hour, they climbed back onto their bikes and headed off.

The next tiny village was run by women, and Dove's skin crawled when the female in charge propositioned him. "I'm married," he muttered.

"Doesn't matter, and I prefer to do my business in bed," she purred.

Revulsion filled him and they made their escape, but not before Jamie made an observation that they likely slept with any man to acquire what they wanted.

By evening they were close to a friendly community and rode inside the gates.

"We're hoping to find a bed for the night. We're trying to talk to those communities who either haven't responded or have declined to participate," Liam told Steven, the man in charge.

Steven cocked his head. "Arguing with fools puts you in a difficult position. Sometimes they're idiots because they just don't know, but others will hold you down and beat you with their experience. You don't want to be confused with either of those, Liam."

Then the man looked over at Dove and he waited, wondering what was required of him in exchange.

"I've got a couple that wants to get married. Don't suppose you have your trappings on hand?" Steven asked.

Dove shook his head. "No, but I can still marry them just the same. Is that all you need?"

Steven tugged at his graying red goatee and huffed. "Got a baptism too, but that can wait 'til you next make rounds." He directed them to a small cabin beside his own. "I got the boys to do it up for the visitors we just seem to keep getting. Dinner is just after nightfall, as you know, and Dove, that would be the time to marry these youngsters."

They entered the rudimentary building and took in the two stark rooms, each holding a bunk bed, and Dove laughed. "Reminds me of the worker's quarters on my father's sheep farm. They were converted from old shipping containers."

They weren't luxurious, but at least they wouldn't have to share a bed, thought Dove, and slid his pack onto the bottom bunk as Liam stared at the accommodation offered.

"You haven't really been out and about much since I came, so I guess you didn't realize some of the conditions people are living in," Dove said.

"Yeah, something like that. Look, I want to talk with Steven after dinner…"

Dove stared at him. "They don't tend to stay up late. Unlike us, they're a bit less evolved in their housing setup. Have very little power."

Liam nodded. "I guess I'm just now starting to realize how lucky we are to have what we do. We scavenged after the first wave and started to build the community from what we had, and we haven't really gone without."

"They don't begrudge us what we have. They have a great sense of family here. Everything is shared down to the child rearing, but they live different lives." Dove needed Liam to understand why some were less welcoming of their visits than others. "It's why some aren't interested. Some have jealousies, others want to live a more traditional lifestyle. I understand why it frustrates you, but they've been cut off since the zombies attacked over two years ago, and they like it that way." He shrugged. "Understanding these people is like understanding women and hormones."

Liam barked out a laugh. "You're telling me! Elaine was always straight forward, at least until before she got pregnant. Now she's a bundle of emotions. Wait 'til it's your turn."

Dove ran a hand through his hair. "Well, I'm sure we'll be waiting a while."

THE MORNING DOVE was meant to return, Leonie was sitting in their tiny lounge, listening to a woman complaining that Elaine and Liam got the best house, the pick of everything, and it wasn't fair.

"Fran, the reason they have that house is that Elaine's grandmother left it to her. I asked about the situation, and that happened well before the zombies. As to why they have the pick, I don't believe that's the case. You brought your concerns to me, and I understand you're feeling stressed and emotional, but—"

The woman launched up out of the seat, her face tight. "No, you don't. You turn up here, marry the priest, and that gives you some kind of superiority complex." Fran lurched for the door and wrenched it open. "You'll get yours!" The waspish words hit home as Leonie jerked back.

Fran wasn't the first, nor would she be the last, she concluded. Rubbing a hand over her aching brow, she wrote down the things she'd said and the comments from Fran. It would be important if the woman decided to 'take matters into her own hands', as she'd threatened to do in the first meeting.

Leonie's notes filled pages, and she rose, heading for the kitchen area. A cup of coffee might calm her nerves, she thought, and she'd just set the kettle on the stove top when the door opened.

She turned, wondering who she had to talk to next, when her gaze fell onto a beloved face. She moved forward without any conscious thought, arms extended. When Dove caught her up, he swung her around, and their lips met and clung.

"I missed you so much!" he growled against her mouth.

She felt the twitch and knew he grinned. "I missed you too. So much." This time the flame between them flared bright, the kiss hot and wild.

A knock echoed from the door, and he tugged away, muttering under his breath, "Never any privacy," and she laughed.

Liam strode inside, Elaine following. "We've got an in-principle agreement from most of the communities. Anterrum wants to see you both, then he's urging us to move quickly. Says he's heard rumblings and rumors." Waving his arm, he urged them forward.

"But what about people's problems?" Leonie asked.

Liam grunted at her words. "You can fill me in after, but right now we need to move quickly."

They hurried to the refectory and took seats at the table they'd used before. Allan Anterrum—the man she'd met at the hospital—waited, his fingers tapping on the table. "Ahh, finally."

Liam and Elaine slid into the seats opposite, and Julia and Leroy joined them as Dove and Leonie rounded out the crew.

"So what?" Julia's voice was cool and remote. Leonie wondered about that then remembered Dove having explained that Julia and her stepfather didn't really have a very positive relationship.

"We need Dove and Leonie ready to go in as soon as possible. One of my informers insists that the militia are almost ready to move. They've got quite a stable of zombies and are ready to release them, then follow behind."

Dove squinted down at the map Allan slid onto the tabletop. "You want intelligence but aren't willing to give us time to prepare?"

Leonie shivered at the suppressed fury in his voice.

"I have people on the inside, Dove. They've been taking chances for a long while. Their information is good, and they can assist to smooth the way. They've indicated they've been agitating from within for some religion. This is where you come in. If you can't do it though…" The words trailed off.

Leonie's fingers curled into claws. "He can, but the danger is extreme. If they work out where he's come from…"

"It won't matter. They know who he is. Where he's from. They'll be counting on—"

Liam held up a hand. "Hang on, what do you mean they know? That will place the two of them in further danger."

Anterrum shook his head. "No, not really. He's a priest and a medic. They know he doesn't fight, and to be honest, my people have been pushing hard on the confidentiality angle. That's how we're getting them in there."

Leonie didn't want to know how they got the information out, but what did worry her was what would happen after they'd finished. Would the militia simply let them go? Did anyone really believe that could be the case?

"Hang on. So, once the job is done, and once we've given them what they need, you expect them to calmly let us out of there?" Derision filled her voice, and Anterrum frowned at her.

Then he smiled. "Yes and no. I would imagine they'll keep you secured in a location far away from what we need to see. One of my operatives will get images to you. I don't know how or in what format though. They'll have what we need to know so we can make arrangements." Anterrum dismissed her by turning back to Liam. "I've also received contact via a short-wave radio from New Zealand. They've become aware that we're attempting to deal with the zombie threat. While they can't send people in, they are hoping to learn about the bases, what armaments are there. They have suggested a United Nations Strike Force to assist in dealing with the threat."

Leonie gasped. Communications with the outside world? Could that really occur? Might they have a chance to once more live a normal life without armed guards following them to ensure their safety outside the fences?

"They can't get involved until they have information. We can't gather our forces either and attack until we have the same intelligence. A lot is riding on you two. Can you do this?"

Anterrum stared at both herself and Dove. Her stomach pitched, and for a moment, her fears almost overtook her. She shook her head to clear away the malaise that settled there. "I'm good. Dove?"

His hand gripped hers. Firm. Assured. "We can do this. We'll leave in the morning."

"Good. Liam's people will take you to this location." Anterrum slid the map close to himself and circled a point on it. "You will then hike to here." He dotted a line to a black square he'd obviously drawn in ink earlier. "You'll be met and searched, so no recording devices or cameras. Once you're cleared, they'll take you inside. We anticipate you'll only be there overnight. After you've completed what you're there to do, I imagine they'll search you and your things again, then you're to be released in this area. Liam's people will be there to collect you and get you out quickly. But while inside, you're functionally on your own—no one will be able to help you, so you'll have to be on your guard the whole time. Wherever they bed you down, remember it will likely be under surveillance."

She gulped, and her fingers tightened on Dove's. *Alone.* Terror slid its fingers down her spine like a trickle of cold water. Only the strength of Dove's hand kept her in place.

"Fine. We'll pack for two days but keep it light. I'll have my travel bag, and apart from that…" He shrugged. "We'll be fine."

Dove tugged her up and away from the table, and they retreated to their home. Once the door shut behind them, she welcomed the calm and quiet.

They didn't speak, merely turned to each other and allowed themselves to embrace. As their lips touched, their hands clasped together.

With slow and sensuous movements, he steered her backward against the door. She rested against the wood, and his mouth roamed across her jaw, feathering light, drugging kisses as he moved.

"Oh, Dove," she muttered, feeling the zing of arousal in her body. In the base of her belly a warm ball of need was growing.

Now comfortable enough to let her hands roam, she slid questing fingers beneath the cotton t-shirt he wore and found hard, hot flesh.

He groaned and moved against her, and her stance changed; widened to allow him access to all of her body.

Dove's hand dove beneath the light band of elastic that held her pants in place, then toyed with the cotton panties she wore.

"So damned hot," he crooned, and she undulated, her breasts firm and ripe for him.

"Touch me," she urged, and his hand slid further, finding the thatch of hair covering her mons. His fingers moved, spearing between the lips of her pussy, and when he found the pearl of her clitoris, she bucked.

"I want you so badly," he whispered against her ear, and the twin need inside her rose. Swamped her.

Her fingers moved without her even thinking, tugging at his shirt. He reared away to help her lift it over his head, then his glorious chest was bared to her gaze. One hand moved to his pecs, covering the nipple and glorying in the wild beat of his heart.

With the other hand, Leonie played with the clasp of his belt, tugging until it came loose. She felt it swing against her belly as he toyed and played.

The button proved irritatingly stubborn, and he pulled away with a dark laugh. "Let me," he ground out, and a shiver wracked her system. She watched as his hands reached for the button, slid it free, then the hiss of the zipper filled the air.

Something deep inside her clenched, and she tensed her legs, needing to stave off the orgasm she knew would explode soon.

With clumsy movements, she stripped off her bottoms as his jeans and underwear dropped to the floor. Her t-shirt followed suit, and the swing of her breasts, next to be released from the confinement of her bra, and the caress of cool air budded her nipples tightly. She hissed in reaction, her eyes closing as her head drew back.

"So beautiful." He cupped a breast, ran his thumb over the beaded tip, and her eyes closed, unable to cope with the sensations that flooded her system.

"Please," she whispered, and he lifted her up.

His erection, long and thick, nudged intimately at her, and she hissed. Wanting and needing him. The fullness she knew that would tip her beyond the realms of reality.

The wire twisting inside her, demanding he fill her, had her winding her legs around his waist, his hands gripping the flesh of her sides.

He slid deep, and she groaned, the sound guttural and primal at the same time. "Please. Dove."

"Yes," he ground against her. "I want you. I love you." The refrain continued with each harsh and demanding move he made.

Leonie held tight, the climax nearing like a tsunami, and she welcomed it. Screamed his name as the breath inside her melted away.

He moved, she knew he did, but she was riding the wave of pleasure. When he came, her eyes opened and she saw the corded neck, the closed eyes, and felt the tremors that wracked his body. "My Leonie," he muttered, and that completed her.

They stayed still, joined in the most intimate of ways as the heat of her skin cooled and the wild beat of her heart slowed.

Limbs growing heavy, she dropped her legs away from him, and Dove slid her down his body. "It's always amazing," he whispered. "I love you."

With a shaking hand, Leonie cupped his cheek. "I'm so lucky to have you, Dove. I would go anywhere with you."

He kissed the palm of her hand and drew her close, into his arms. "We should shower and eat. Early morning ahead of us." Just like that the afterglow of amazing sex melted away and once more her fears assailed. He tugged at her, but she remained still, until he looked back, a question in his eyes.

"Dove? I'm afraid."

His gaze searched her face. "You can stay here. I can go alone."

Shaking her head, Leonie searched for the words to explain. "No. I want to come with you, but I don't want to make a mistake. What we'll see may upset me, and I may open my mouth."

"So could I. But I'm glad you're coming with me. I really want you there, because as stupid as it sounds, I think it's the best way for our mission to be successful."

"Then I guess we should pack."

He nodded but waited a beat longer. "Shower first though?"

There was suggestion in his tone, and she laughed, tapped him on the shoulder. "You're such a lech for a priest!" It only occurred to her later that he'd chosen those words to settle her nerves.

Chapter 15

Dove waited for Leonie to catch up. She breathed hard from the exertion of hiking their way toward the entry of the militia base. They needed to increase their pace, but he was all too aware she was struggling with the trek after they'd been dropped off at the agreed zone.

He wondered, not for the first time, how the agreement had come about. After all, they were from a camp the militia was trying to wipe out, yet, they'd agreed to his and Leonie's presence. Had there been some kind of payment?

"I'm sorry I'm slowing you down," Leonie panted, and he took her hand.

"Have a drink of water and we'll take a break."

Leonie shook her head. "No, we need to keep going. Get to where we're going before nightfall."

His estimation of her rose about one hundred percent again, but he slowed his steps, watching as she occasionally limped. "Hurt your feet?"

"No, they've just rubbed a little. I'll be fine."

He wanted to hiss they would be alright, but it would be an

untruth. Just before leaving the camp, Anterrum had rounded him up.

"They've agreed to allow safe passage for you to their camp, but you're going to have to move quickly. You must be within by four PM, otherwise they'll lock you out and we won't be able to get to you."

A glance at his watch told him it was nearly three now. He could see the building ahead, the ground around it cleared of vegetation. No crops or animals roamed. There were just miles of endless stumps.

"We're going to have to move faster to make it there in time," he urged, and she sighed.

"I know."

Dove took her hand, and they entered the large cleared zone, having exited the stand of trees they'd used for cover. *At least it's not high summer.* That would have made the trek unbearable.

They'd crouched down, out of sight, to take a sip of water from a bottle when a sound turned his guts to frozen slush. The low, moaning dirge of a zombie.

"We have to get out of here."

He tugged and pulled her along, and they flew over the ground, stumbling and panting.

The sounds of fear coming from her tore at him, but there was no time. They entered the bush and they crunched their way onward. Anything to get away to safety.

He glanced back, noting two more had joined the chase. "We have…to keep…going," he panted.

Where are we? This made no sense. Anterrum had been so sure the informant would meet them.

Dove tripped, his foot sliding into a dip in the ground, and he fell. His head cracked loudly as it made contact with the ground.

Leonie squealed, her eyes wide. "Oh no! Dove, get up."

The shooting pain in his leg was an indication he'd done serious damage to himself, and though he tried to rise, the leg he'd fallen on was caught fast. Pain spiraled, and his mind spun in a million circles, each tighter than the last as reality crashed down.

In the middle of nowhere. Zombies after them and no way to defend themselves.

Face facts, Dove. Send her away now!

The ice in his belly slid through his limbs. "I'm trapped, Leonie."

His wife crouched beside him, her hands moving like butterflies, darting here and there without any real use. "We have to get out of here," she whispered, her gaze on the bush behind her.

Dove shook his head. "I'm stuck."

"What?" Now her head turned, her eyes on him. He could see the horror dawning on her face. "No. I'll get you out of here."

She made to rise, but he caught her hand, demanding she listen. "You have to go."

"No. Don't ask that of me." The set of her mouth, the defiance that settled over her like a mantle filled him with both joy and sadness.

"You have to save yourself." The pain in his leg was turning his mind fuzzy, and blackness edged his vision.

"No way. I'm not leaving, Dove. Let me see how badly…" Her voice trailed away, and she glanced around wildly.

The sound of approaching movement caught his ears. *How to make her leave?* His thinking was in snatches now, disjointed and getting harder.

"Please. Go." He closed his eyes, stomach lurching, and dizziness assailed him. He couldn't open them, but heard movement and wanted to scream at the unfairness of it all. *How could this happen? Why, God?* Then the thoughts, like his consciousness, fled.

ALONE. Dove had passed out, his face white and beaded with moisture. Leonie would protect him if it were the last thing she'd ever do.

Her gaze fell on a small limb, obviously fallen during a storm, that lay on the ground. It was large enough to do damage yet not too weighty for her to wield.

The sounds of feet, tramping and crunching on the leaves, grew louder, and she took up a stance, limb over her shoulder. *Good thing I liked softball.* She held onto the small bit of humor and let it ground her in reality, because what she really wanted to do right now was drop to the ground and scream for help.

Tears stung her eyes, and fear closed like a vise around her chest.

The sound of movement was clearer and louder. Her hands sweated, but she gripped that wood. *Our lives depend on this*, she thought.

"Dove?" a voice called, and Leonie gritted her teeth, breathing as quietly as she could though the wild run still had adrenaline coursing through her body. "Dove? I'm here to help."

Her mind was sluggish, but reality hit home suddenly. *Talking. Not a zombie.*

But who could this be, she wondered, not knowing the woman's voice.

The sounds changed direction as if leaving her, and she realized if this person left, they'd be alone and stranded. At the mercy of whatever chased them. "Here," Leonie called, all the while hoping she'd made the right decision.

The footsteps stopped. "Dove?"

"Over here," she called as her eyes scanned the bush, still wary of zombies out there.

She bit her lip as two women emerged from the darkness, dressed in fatigues, small pistols in their hands. "What the hell happened?" one demanded while the other crouched beside Dove.

"He's going to need an evac," stated the other, older woman, her gaze and hands assessing Dove and his injury. "I'm Ellen and this is Cherie."

Tears dribbled down Leonie's cheek, and she dropped the limb. If they weren't here to help, the limb would be little assistance in protecting either of them. "Zombies. They were following us."

Ellen advanced, and while it felt like quicksand had invaded her veins, Leonie stood her ground.

"We saw them. They escaped the facility, or more likely were released, after we snuck out to find you two. The situation's changed, and they'll kill us if they can find us. We need to get away from here," Ellen muttered.

Cherie, crouching beside Dove, coughed, and both Leonie and Ellen turned. "He's not in a good way. We need to get his leg out of the hole then splinted. The only way we're going to get him out of here is to create a pallet and drag him. We're not far from the car, but we'll have to work quickly."

Leonie didn't know if she trusted the woman or not, but the fact was, he needed help of the kind she wasn't capable of giving.

Ellen turned, whipped off her backpack, and opened it. Scrabbling inside, she took out a tool. It looked like a survivalist item, but unfolded into a rudimentary shovel. "Cherie, help me dig him out. And you," she said and indicated to Leonie, "bring me a couple of straight sticks, then see if you can find a few more limbs like that." She pointed to the one Leonie had dropped on the ground.

The two women set to work, and for a second, Leonie stood there, stock-still and shocked, then she complied.

There have been storms through here recently, she thought as she stayed close and found what she'd been ordered to seek. Hurrying back to Dove, she watched the woman straighten and splint his leg. Swelling and bruising were already evident.

Under instruction, she scrabbled through her bag, found shirts and tied the larger pieces of wood together, then lay it down next to Dove. Ellen tugged his bag off and shoved it to the side, as if she was going to leave it there, and Leonie shrugged hers off. "I'll take that."

Both women stared at her as if she'd run mad. "We're going to have to leave it all behind," Ellen told her.

Leonie shook her head. "No. We won't leave it behind. I'll help and carry it out."

Once they'd fastened Dove to the pallet they stood up and the women took the lead, dragging him together while Leonie followed behind to keep an eye out.

The ground was rough, and more than once he was jounced, and Leonie would wince, thankful he was still unconscious but also fearful because his injury was serious enough to keep him out cold.

Night was falling as they came upon a deeper copse, hiding a tarpaulin-covered shape.

"Cover me," Ellen muttered and moved closer. Leonie remained by Dove, watching as the tarp was ripped aside, then the woman peered inside the vehicle. "It's safe."

They opened the doors of the old car, and between the three of them, they hustled Dove inside and laid him across the backseat. Leonie clambered in and shoved Dove's bag down into the footpace.

"We need to move, Ellen," growled Cherie as she tried to start the car. The *click click click* of the engine sent Leonie's throat into her mouth, the sound of dogs and moans now echoing.

Ellen snatched up a hammer, popped the bonnet, and with two sharp cracks, hit something in the motor.

"What's she—" Leonie said, but was cut off.

"Shhh…"

Ellen slid back into the car, bonnet once more firmly closed, and Cherie tried the ignition again. This time it fired, and they were reversing out of the hidden area.

"This could get messy, so stay down," warned Ellen, and they turned, shot out of the section and onto a small track, little more than a tire track in the middle of nowhere.

"Where are we going?"

"To the nearest safe settlement," Cherie answered, her face tight as they drove through the deepening dusk. "We can't turn the lights on yet, so I'll talk later when I don't have to concentrate so hard."

Leonie glanced down at Dove, noting his eyes were open, his face tight and white. "Dove?"

"I'm going to be sick," he groaned and proceeded to do so.

The scent of vomit filled the air, sour, and her fear ratcheted up. "Is this normal?"

Cherie, who'd ministered to him, turned her gaze from the road and narrowed her eyes. "Head hurts?"

"Oh yes," he whispered, head thrust back against the padding of the seat, eyes closed again.

"Do you know who the woman beside you is?" She snuck a quick look at the road then back to them.

He laughed, then it cut short as he hissed and grabbed Leonie's hand. "My wife."

Cherie looked at her, frowned, then nodded. "Okay. I think you may have a concussion, so I need you to stay awake for me. How's the leg?"

"Hurts," he moaned, and Leonie's stomach shrank in fright, her gaze on his face.

"Is he going to be all right?"

Cherie answered her question with, "He needs a doctor and medical attention. The leg isn't in a good way, but it's the concussion right now that worries me most." She turned forward, and Leonie silently urged her to go faster.

"Keep him awake."

Leonie nodded, and her head spun. They'd been lucky, but surely, they'd manage to hold on a little longer.

The vehicle rocked and rolled, and Leonie couldn't forget the older cars she and her brother had driven earlier in their lives, farm vehicles that in hindsight, probably weren't the safest choices, but what they'd both learned to drive in.

After one particularly nasty bump, where Dove cried out, she cradled his head. "We'll be there soon," she crooned then looked up. "How long?"

The woman driving cast her a glance over her shoulder. "Not long now."

Leonie had to admit to a feeling of relief when the sight of the gates of their own community came into view. They opened, and the car moved inside.

"Take the right track and follow it through. Watch for kids," Leonie urged.

They drove right up to the hospital, and she waited until two orderlies rushed out, took one look at Dove, and called for Ramon. Dove's face was tight with pain, and Ramon ordered a gurney tugged up beside the car then assisted in lifting Dove out of the car and onto the bed.

"He'll be all right, won't he?" She wrung her hands, hoping for reassurance, but he gave her a non-committal look.

"Go see Elaine and Liam. Report to them then come back. I should have a better idea by then," Ramon answered almost absently.

Shoving her hands deep into the pockets of her pants, Leonie watched as they wheeled Dove into the examination room and shut the door. She whirled. "What the hell is going on?" Fury and fright congealed inside her and suddenly she needed answers.

"We need to talk with Anterrum," Ellen stated.

"Why?" Leonie shot back, and the woman's eyes squeezed shut. "Look, that's my husband in there. He nearly died today, and I deserve to know what the hell is going on." The angrier she became, the higher the pitch of her voice, and both women winced.

The door opened and Ramon gazed out. "Take it somewhere else and let me do my job."

Leonie firmed her lips. "Follow me," she hissed, and they followed, the heat of their gazes burning on the back of her neck.

She rapped on Liam and Elaine's door and entered when called forward. His face turned slack with shock when he saw her.

Anterrum rose and marched toward them. "What the hell is going on?"

The woman in charge of the two, Ellen, pushed inside. "They've worked out that we've been passing information to you, and even worse, they're planning to attack. I've got info, notes, and maps." The rip of Velcro filled the air, and Leonie waited, seething.

Liam glanced at her. "Where's Dove?"

"With Ramon. He has a badly broken leg, according to Ellen, and a concussion. God knows what else." Angry tears pricked, but she blinked them away, refusing to give in here, before these women and Anterrum.

Elaine hurried forward and hugged her.

For a moment, Leonie remained stiff, then her control slipped. "I was so afraid," she whispered, and Elaine held her tight.

"We'll check on him soon. What did Ramon say?" Liam placed a warm hand on her shoulder, and Leonie sighed.

"To bring them here, then return and he'd have a better idea."

"I'll go with her." Elaine released Leonie and turned to Liam.

"Isla's asleep and changed. You should have a while. When we're done, I'll send word or come home." She then urged Leonie from the house and together they returned to the hospital.

They'd barely entered when Ramon met them in the waiting room. "Oh good. Leonie, Dove does have a concussion, and he'll need to stay here tonight. He also has a fracture of both the tibia and fibula. They are clean breaks and quite stable, so that's something, but he's going to have to be in a cast for the next six weeks, then we'll take a look at how it's healing."

"But the bruising and swelling? There was nothing else…"

Ramon smiled. "It's normal in breaks for that to happen. He's had a rough time but should heal well. I've got a nurse applying his cast right now, so once that's done you can come on in."

The weight on her chest lifted. "Good. That's great."

A sudden wave of vertigo hit, and she swayed, the room tilting a little.

"Let's get you onto a chair," Ramon said as he steered Leonie to a seat. She sat heavily and waited for the unfamiliar sensation to pass. "When did you last eat?"

She glanced up through her lashes. "I… I don't know. Lunchtime, I guess."

Ramon sent Elaine to find food and water, then he slid into the seat beside Leonie. "First time?"

She started to nod but stilled when the room twirled before her eyes.

"Any injuries? Bites?" He flashed a light in her eyes.

"No. None."

Elaine returned with a sandwich and water, and Leonie ate slowly, letting the food fill her stomach. "What about Dove?"

Ramon smiled. "He'll be fed once he's on the ward. But if you'll come into my office for a moment?" He stood and Leonie followed him into the tiny room, leaving Elaine behind with a, "Thanks, but you should go home now."

Settling in the uncomfortable chair, she watched as he rifled through the drawer and pulled out a small file with her name on it. "So, when was your last period?"

Her mouth dropped open.

Chapter 16

Returning home was an anti-climax, concluded Dove. Liam and Ramon, Leroy and Elaine, together with Julia and Leonie made sure he was comfortable on the lounge, his leg raised. Books materialized beside it, along with glasses of cool water and home-made lemonade.

On the third day, Anterrum paid him a visit.

"So, you seem to be making a full recovery," Anterrum commented, lowering himself into one of the two armchairs while Leonie bustled about the kitchen.

She hummed as she baked bread and scones. She'd even made a creditable damper for their supper to go with the stew that always seemed to be on the menu.

"That's what the doctor told me," Dove answered, but it was a wary comment, and he wondered what Anterrum really wanted.

The man settled back in the chair, his gaze on Leonie. "I'm thinking you consider yourself entitled to an explanation of what happened the other day at the militia camp?"

Dove heard Leonie still, the slide of a tray on the benchtop. "I think so, Mr. Anterrum. Dove wouldn't have been injured, and we wouldn't have been terrified, if more information had been forthcoming." The sound of her measured steps as she came toward them was loud in the silence.

"Well, what we didn't know at the time is that the operator who'd been making contact with the New Zealand officials had been passing on information concerning the situation. When we sent you into the militia zone, we expected that we'd need intelligence, but the two women, Ellen and Cherie, got wind that the messages were being intercepted. They also realized their cover was blown, so grabbed what they could and headed out."

Leonie sat on the arm of Dove's seat, and he caught her around the waist. "So?"

"New Zealand has been advocating for a year or more to form a strike force. Once they knew what the reason behind the zombies were, they understood that if the people behind the situation here got their information out to others, no country would be safe. The impure vaccine could be employed any time and any place."

That nugget of information fell between them like a heavy weight. "They need to stop them," Dove guessed.

Anterrum nodded. "Yes. They're going to drop a UN Force in to deal with the militia. Starting here and moving to all the capital centers before fanning out. The first drop is expected tonight. Liam has been clearing the old sports fields and will have guards on high alert."

"So, what happens then?" Leonie entwined her fingers with Dove's and gripped tight.

"Oww," he yelped, feeling the pinch.

"Sorry." She loosened her grip.

The smile Anterrum gave him reminded him of a crocodile he'd once seen in Far North Queensland. "We re-establish the government and gather whatever police and armed forces we can. There'll be a period of adjustment, and likely martial law, but with control, we can once again open our borders."

"But the zombies," she breathed.

His smile died. "There's not many options. We catch them, but with them in confinement we'll likely have a bloodbath. We have to put them out of their misery. It's the only way we'll regain control."

Dove's heart lurched. "But surely there must be something else we can do?"

"No vaccines we've tried have worked, and we've seen the mutations speeding up. We can't let them gain total control or they'll wipe out the population." His face turned grim. "There are no other options. I've been in contact with friends in other states, and their findings are the same. We've got the worst of it down here, and we believe the militia thought they had us cowed and it's why the situation here has been so bad. They may have released the initial doses nationally, but they focused on the wrong group of people."

Anterrum paused a moment as he rose.

"When this is done, there are people from most of the camps we want to talk to about taking on positions of leadership. Dove, you've impressed me with your calmness and ability to talk rationally. You and your wife have handled the situation with the militia well, and would make excellent ambassadors." He smiled and moved to the door. "Think on that."

Once Anterrum had left, Dove tugged her close and kissed her, feeling once more the burn of passion. "We could..." He waggled his eyebrows.

She laughed, and he was pleased to note the shadows that had settled in her eyes gradually lightening. Leonie had lost so much, and he was damned pleased she wasn't losing anything else important to her. Including, and especially, him.

Pulling away with a gentle sigh, she put a hand against his chest. "Dove I..."

A knock at the door echoed, and she rolled her eyes, rose, and opened the door.

Liam burst in. "Come on, you're going to want to see this."

Liam pushed the wheelchair Ramon had lent them to the chair where Dove reclined. Having found the crutches still a little bit difficult to navigate, Dove climbed in the wheelchair, Leonie taking control and pushing him through the door.

They headed for the field, and Liam ensured a path was cleared for him to watch. The growing roar of aircraft had them all looking up, and dots that gradually grew larger filled their vision. Soon, they were large enough to make out the parachutes, and excitement filled him.

Liam and his wife stood side by side, he taking Isla while Elaine snapped photos. "For posterity," she said with a laugh.

Children who'd seen too much clung to their parents or caregivers in fear while the teens cheered.

It seemed to take forever for the men and women who'd been dropped from the aircraft to make their landing, but soon a wall of mottled gray and green suited men and women formed up, the leader striding toward them.

"I'm looking for Liam?" The woman was large and dark-skinned, her eyes shone with a brown light, and her hair was ruthlessly tied back. "I'm Major Brigham."

His leg might be aching, but he wouldn't miss this for the world, Dove thought, and once again marveled that they'd survived to see the initial strike force arrive.

Introductions were made and the major looked at him in the chair. "Father," she called him, and he almost laughed at the incongruity of it. No one had called him that in so long. Everyone simply knew him as Dove.

Liam set about delegating tasks, arrangements for meals would be dealt with by Elaine's assistant, Hannah, then they headed for the refectory.

The major, striding ahead, looked left and right. "It's amazing what you've done under the circumstances. We had heard there are other communities here, but they don't have the same kind of infrastructure."

Dove chimed in, "Liam and his wife, Elaine, were here when it all began. His brother is a doctor, and he was a policeman beforehand. They took the situation in hand, arranged the teams to track down what they needed, and so this came about."

Liam offered him a shocked look. "I didn't realize you knew—"

Leonie laughed. "He's a priest. People tell him things all the time."

"True that," Dove added as they tugged a chair out so he could slide into the end of the table, and Leonie settled on the side nearest his leg.

The ubiquitous stew was delivered in bowls and spoons found, while large hunks of bread were placed in platters.

Once more the major looked at what was offered. "You have meat and vegetables?"

"We farm, to feed ourselves and to barter for goods at other camps. We have our own butcher, and we're pretty close to self-sufficient." Liam shrugged. "Lighting and electricity are created by solar panels, and we had electricians in the early days assist in increasing our generation. Water comes from a bore behind some of the original houses. It too is solar driven, and we managed to hunt down some batteries in the early days so we have enough to make do when there is little to no sunlight."

"Amazing," she breathed, and the other officers who'd joined them nodded in agreement.

"The sports grounds are yours for as long as you need them for your temporary base. I've also got copies of maps showing where we know the militia are encamped."

"How?" Surprise colored the major's question, and Liam smiled.

"We're very resourceful. We found photocopiers and paper. It's made our life a little easier. We also have our own Births, Deaths, and Marriages, so down the track we can assist those seeking to reunite with families or share information on those we know were lost."

The woman shook her head. "Resourceful my ass." But there was humor in the comment, so they simply ignored it.

"Dove, before we begin, would you mind saying grace?" asked Elaine, and they bowed their heads.

"Lord, we give thanks for the food you've given us, the friendships and families we've formed, and the opportunity to do what we can to assist in bringing stability and hope to those who've waited patiently. We thank you for your love and generosity. Amen."

A chorus of *amen*s wafted across the tables, and as they ate they recalled snippets of information, the outline of plans, and who would be left behind at base to coordinate. After the meal was over, Ramon wandered in and pulled Elaine to the side. She smiled broadly and excused herself. "Isla is fussing after we sent her to Uncle Ramon. Gotta go."

As Ramon and Elaine left, Dove slanted a look at Leonie, and his gaze narrowed.

"Everything okay?"

Leonie smiled nervously. "Never better, why?"

He didn't miss that she turned away, but he let it ride. For now. But Ramon was a doctor, and it appeared to Dove that there was something she was keeping from him. He didn't like secrets much, especially of the medical variety.

As the party split up, Leonie took control of the wheelchair. "Let's take a walk."

He remained quiet, aware she was carrying some kind of load. They reached the side of the camp where they could watch the workers in the fields, and there she stopped, applied the brakes, and still he waited.

Leonie settled herself on the ground before him, her hand reaching for his. She inhaled, and the flare of her nostrils and the sudden tension filled him with dread.

"Back at the refectory you asked me if everything was okay, and I tried to talk to you earlier, but there were so many distractions and people coming and going." Her shoulders rose in a shrug. "When we were at the hospital yesterday, I nearly fainted. In front of Ramon. So, he pulled me into his office, and I had an exam. I had to pee on a stick."

She sounded so put out that Dove couldn't contain the tiny grin, but it quickly melted away. A sickly feeling settled inside him.

"And?"

She reached into her pocket, drew out something, and slid it into his hands.

He stared at it, his mind unable to comprehend what this meant. The tiny device showed a single line. He gazed at the plastic in his hands, his mind sluggish. "What does this mean?" Pushing the words past the restriction in his throat made them sound thick, and he looked up at her.

Now she smiled and moved closer. "I'm pregnant, Dove. You're going to be a daddy in about eight and a half months, we think."

"How?"

Her laughter tinkled. "Well, when a man and a woman…"

"Very funny. But we used contraceptive…" Confusion filled his mind again.

"Except by the door, in the shower, and whenever we get a little frisky in a hurry." Leonie ticked the times off on her fingers, then bit her lip and looked down. "You are pleased, right?" Now she sounded sad, as if he'd somehow stood on a kitten or kicked a puppy.

He reached out, wishing he'd thought before opening his mouth. "Very pleased, Leonie, just surprised. Wow. A baby. *Our baby.*" He tugged her close, feeling excitement starting to fizz and pop in his veins.

She moved, jostled his leg, and he moaned with discomfort.

"Ohmygosh! Dove…" Leonie patted him, her face dropping with worry. "Ramon! He'll check if we've bumped anything."

"Wait!" She'd already shot up, ready to move him, and he turned, ignoring the dull throb of his leg and thanked Ramon silently for the pain pills he'd insisted Dove take before releasing him this morning from the hospital. "Leonie, I'm really pleased. Over-joyed, and I should have told you that."

She stopped pushing and stared down at him, his neck cricked so he could scan her face. "You're not just saying the words, are you? I mean, I know we agreed we wanted children, but we haven't discussed it, but…" She inhaled. "I'm over the moon, to be honest. I look at Elaine and Liam and it occurs to me they're happy. They took a chance, and things are improving. What a way to celebrate."

He laughed. "I would imagine we're probably at the front because tonight, I'll be surprised if there aren't lots of little ones started."

Leonie batted his hand. "That's a naughty thing to say."

He grunted. "Maybe, but you mark my words."

Epilogue

Eight and a half months later

"Push, Leonie," Ramon urged, while Dove held tight to her hand. She might be trying to squeeze it dry, but he'd stay by her side if that was the last thing he did, and he wouldn't make a sound, though the pain was blooming.

Leonie's hair stuck to the side of her very red face, and she bore down, "I'm trying!"

"You can do this, sweetheart." Amazement warred with humbleness as she fought for the birth of their child.

She panted and dug deep; one last massive push and the sound of the baby slithering from her body filled the air. Silence stretched then… He glanced to Ramon and a smile split his face as the first wail echoed.

"It's a—"

"No!" Leonie barked and held out her hands.

Ramon carefully passed the baby over to its mother.

She laughed and turned, the pain melting from her face. "A girl. A daughter for us, Dove."

Wonder filled him. The long hours of worry passing as if they hadn't occurred, and he bent down, kissing his wife. "Thank you, Leonie. This gift is the best ever." It truly was, and tears filled his eyes as he gazed upon the two females who meant the world to him.

Ramon stepped up to him. "Want to cut the cord?"

He glanced down, his stomach churning a little, but he took the scissors being held out to him and made the cut separating mother and child. His wife. His daughter.

"Joy will never know anything but happiness," Leonie whispered, and he smiled. *The name so appropriate*, he thought.

Ramon took the baby while the nurses scurried around, helping Leonie to clean up and get a little more comfortable, then Joy was returned to Leonie's arms. "We'll leave you three alone for a while." And the medical staff left the room, not that either of them really noticed.

Dove cuddled Leonie as best he could, though it felt awkward with the bundle between them wrapped in a pink blanket.

Bending his head, he prayed. "Lord, you have given us so much, and baby Joy adds to the gifts. We thank you for her safe delivery and pray for a safe future for her and us as a family. Amen."

The baby squirmed and cried as Leonie levered herself up in the bed, bared her breast, and the baby latched on almost immediately.

He reached out, and the way his daughter grabbed his fingers squeezed his heart.

"Remember all those months ago, when you said that it was as if we'd been brought here to be in the right place and the right time? It all makes sense now." Leonie's voice had him smiling. "I think we were being guided to this point in time, and I can't be thankful enough."

Soon enough the baby dropped off to sleep, and Leonie adjusted her shirt.

Ramon sent them home that afternoon, assuring them he'd be just a call away. Visitors came. Elaine and Liam and Julia and Leroy numbered among them, and Dove marveled at the changes eight months had brought.

Elaine and Liam both sat on the board that assisted in the governing of the region, having had experience in the years since the zombie outbreak occurred.

"How did you get time away?" Leonie enquired, and Liam smiled.

"When you're the chair, you can delegate things. Besides, I had to meet Joy today. Before the news of her arrival spread and your parishioners descended, Dove."

He laughed and pointed to the bench of the kitchen. "They've already heard Leonie was in labor. Take a look." The bench was covered with quiches and stews, roasts, and even cakes. Most of these things unheard of during the worst of the apocalypse.

Booties and mittens, coats, and even knitted baby blankets piled high on the chairs, and Liam chortled. "So okay, we're a bit late to the party."

Elaine peeked over Leonie's shoulder as Isla prattled away in babyspeak, slung from the carrier on her mother's chest. "Look, Isla, a little friend. It won't be long before you're running around together."

"Along with dozens of others. There's going to be a blip this year as celebratory babies pop!" Leonie spoke drily as Julia took up position beside her, the bulk of her own pregnancy making her uncomfortable.

"Huh, well it's not my fault," Julia added, and Dove snickered.

"At least Leroy made your relationship legal before you started to show." Dove laughed.

Leroy grunted. "No baby of mine wasn't going to have my last name. Besides, too many other guys were checking Julia out. Couldn't have that."

Though the words came out with a smile, Dove knew just how big a step it was for Leroy to commit. His PTSD was now being addressed, as an international team of therapists had arrived not long after Canberra had been declared an incident-free zone.

When the door opened again, to admit Ramon, he wasn't alone

either. The woman holding his hand, bronze-skinned and drawling in her American accent. "So, another Aussie to save, I guess." And they all laughed. The major—or Ann as they now knew her—stepped forward. "She's going to be a beauty, if mama and pops are anything to go by."

"Yeah. And here I was, beaten to the woman by a guy who picked her up on a motorbike." The crowd laughed, realizing the words were all too true.

Dove coughed and cleared the air. "So, how is it going, Ramon?"

Ramon sighed. "Well, I thought I'd do the deed right here."

Eyes widened with shock at his words, but then and there Ramon dropped to one knee in front of those assembled, and Dove moved close to his wife and took her hand.

"Ann? You've been here for over eight months. Long enough to know if you plan to stay and have me, so I need to know. Will you marry me?"

Ann stood still for a moment then sighed, the sound loud and dramatic. "What took you so long to ask? Of course, I will. Now get off the floor."

Those assembled laughed and 'congratulations' rang out.

Dove looked over everyone there. Family. He'd realized not long after Leonie came into his life that he wasn't alone anymore. That had filled him with peace, but it was only after she filled his life that he accepted that he'd gained so much more than friends. He'd acquired a family, and that was who gathered today in celebration—his family. And it felt great.

Did you enjoy this book by Imogene Nix?
Feel free to leave a review, join her newsletter and
keep reading to find lots of other books by this author!

Executing Justice
THE REUNION TRILOGY BOOK 3

Kumi Ito has her mission, as does Carmichael Snow, but are their objectives compatible?

Kumi Ito is a woman with a problem. Since assuming the role of head of the Commerce Department, she's found discrepancies… the kind that could cause anarchy if the truth got out.

When Carmichael Snow, the commander of the *Emancipation*, comes across intelligence that someone has placed a hit on Kumi, he has to save her. His plan? Hide her and find the assassin.

As they dodge the killer, a passion ignites between them that runs from simmering all the way to steamy. But will the actions of one snatch away their happiness before they can accept what is growing between them?

Chapter One

Gillian sighed heavily as she leaned her aching head against the bolster. No matter how many different ways she tried to see her brother's—her twin's—choices, there was never anything that made them seem any better. But then, how could it? Her twin, Anderson, had organized a hit on the sister of the man Gillian loved.

"How could you do this?" In the darkness, there was no answer.

She rubbed her brow. Her life was in tatters, just as his was. Her position as the personal assistant to Senator Ito had disappeared like fog on a summer morning, thanks to Anderson's stupid actions. With a conviction against his name, she couldn't access any of the highly confidential information that came with her job. She was now deemed a 'security risk'.

As a result, she'd been dismissed by a chair jockey from the Central Registry of Employment. The CRE oversaw all positions within the government. She didn't like it. Not one bit. All the years she'd worked tirelessly had been dissolved in one pen stroke. But there was no avenue of appeal. So much for natural justice.

"Ugh, why couldn't you have done something else, like…be a baker? Damn it, Anderson." She dragged the pillow over her face to muffle the sound of the words her mother shouldn't hear and to absorb her angry tears. She already had enough to be concerned about, with her only son in the prison system now and her daughter unable to secure a job.

"Gillian, dear? Is everything okay?" The querulous sound of her mother's voice from the next bedroom had her sitting up and sighing.

"Yeah, everything is fine, Ma. You go to sleep."

Gillian listened for the rustling sound of her mother settling in her bed. The worst part was that she missed her boss. The job had been great, acting as his executive assistant had brought with it a range of experiences. But it was the time spent in his company that had given her the most satisfaction and fulfillment. Tomi. If she closed her eyes, she could see him in her mind. Toned and golden brown, with a hint of the orient in the slant of his eyes.

She huffed in the silence. "Now there'll be no more of that." With the thought came a pang of loss. Another salty tear traced its way down her face. She brushed it away. "No use in crying over what can never be." But between Anderson's actions and Tomi's lack of contact, her life felt like little more than a pile of ashes. The introspection didn't stop the pain that wracked her system. Glancing out the window, she could see the moon high in the sky.

"I wonder if he is looking at the same moon and wondering about me." Gillian cursed herself for her foolish thoughts before slumping back into the bedcovers.

She dragged the pillow under her head and turned away from the window. I should get some sleep. Tomorrow I'll need to look for work. Her heart still ached as she closed her eyes and let sleep claim her.

Available in Ebook
https://books2read.com/ExecutingJustice

Direct Autographed Copy (The Reunion Trilogy)
https://bit.ly/reuniontrilogy

Miss Isabelle's Craving
THE SEARCH DUOLOGY BOOK 2

Two sisters, one driving desire for passion.

After her sister's successful marriage, Isabelle Forster is sure she'll only ever be an old maid aunt. That is until she meets Langdon Deveraux. He's tall, he's dashing, and he excites her enough to take a walk on the wild side. But with only a month to explore Shanghai before her sister and brother-in-law have decreed they must return to England, time is short.

Langdon wants Isabelle from the first moment they meet, but with the news that she's leaving shortly, he's propelled into action after she makes an advance that leaves him reeling. Marriage is the only answer, but he's got other pressing issues: hunting down the opium importers and pressure from his superior to see if the Forster sisters are involved.

Between the opium problem and issues with running Forster Shipping, Isabelle is learning to accept her sexuality and changed circumstances. It's going to make the first weeks of marriage full of adventure and danger.

Chapter One

Isabelle's hand hovered over her journal page, the fountain pen—a relatively new invention—sitting just above the heavy paper.

January 1879
It's been difficult since my illness in Calcutta and Bombay. I have had
so few opportunities to write openly about the time since we left
England. Even though we are now bound for Shanghai, and quite close
according to the captain, my excitement is dimmed. I fear my illness
returning, and though I have Jacinthe here, the thought of any further
debilitation fills me with dread.
I find the long hours of this voyage taxing—the hours without actual
occupation tedious. Without much to do, I read and draw, yet I yearn
for something to capture my attention. A way to fill my mind, so I may
rest easy.
In the darkness of night, I also find myself fearing the sounds I some-

times hear emanating from the cabin next to me. The one Aeddan and Elspeth share.

They do try to be quiet, but sometimes, I cannot help but hear. I am not unaware of the hungers of the flesh.

The pen rose as Isabelle looked toward the open window. It wasn't easy to pour out the myriad of fears that filled her mind.

When I was younger, I'd listen to the housemaids' chatter. It didn't seem to be pleasurable then with the talk of heat and fury, but now I hear Elspeth, and I wonder at the glow I see on her face. The joy that radiates from her daily.

I am genuinely pleased for my sister, but for myself, there is nothing but despair.

Perhaps it is the knowledge that Louisa is married and expecting her first child and Elspeth is happy with her choice.

Truly, Aeddan is a perfect foil for Elspeth, and the jealousy I feel sickens me. He is good. Attentive and kind. Resourceful and loving. Everything she deserves.

In my future, I see nothing similar.

No possibility of the pleasure I cannot sometimes escape the echoes of. What if that is all that exists? A spinsterhood that stretches into the future? It's not enough.

I should learn to be content.

I will strive tomorrow to be more. To find an inner well of self-containment, but I fear this is not a skill I possess.

I

Scrubbing at her eyes, Isabelle sighed, blew softly on the page then sanded it so the ink wouldn't bleed, before closing the leather cover of her diary. Jacinthe snored lightly in the bunk on the other side of the cabin as the vessel swayed gently.

Isabelle reached over and placed the diary on the trunk beside her bed and turned the knob, extinguishing the lamp. She lay down, gaze settled on the horizon, the blanket pulled closer against the cold breeze. Moonlight filtered in through the open window, and she lay there a long time contemplating it before finally giving in to slumber.

Available in Ebook
https://books2read.com/MissIsabelle

Direct Autographed Copy
https://bit.ly/IsabelleCraving

The Blood Bride by Imogene Nix

Hope just wants to be an ordinary nestling. She went to college and escaped, but now she's back and there's a secret everyone is keeping from her.

Xavier is the new master of the nest, ready to welcome home the daughter of the house who he has never met. He's unprepared for the woman who steals his breath and enchants him.

Now Hope and Xavier must fight for lives and those of the innocents. After all, it is only by overcoming the rogues that they will have a chance of a timeless future together. But will it be in time?

PROLOGUE

As silence descended on the house, the shadows grew—dark grays and blacks that bled into each other. First one figure then another broke away, making a run toward the house. Silent as the grave, they moved swiftly over dew-slicked grass. Then they stopped still. Waiting. Not a movement betrayed them until a signal propelled them back into action and they started crawling upwards. The walls damp coating no barrier to the intruders that ascended in the darkness.

The sound of each window breaking shattered the quiet—the figures were inside. Screams echoed through the night. Yet, in this area of large estates, heavy with noise-absorbing shrubbery, no one could hear those within. The blood-curdling screams went on and on before finally dying away.

Just one sound echoed through the night: The sobbing of a child.

The front door opened and figures trooped out—ghostly specters against an inky night sky, broken by a single outline. A child in white, carried at the center of the pack.

No sound broke the silence as they moved toward the trees surrounded the house.

Flames now licked at the manor: A deathly glow of oily smoke rising.

All that remained was a single person—wrapped in a cape of midnight blue beyond the house—watching them melt away.

Jemima moved toward the burning structure, breaking into a run as she breached the threshold. Vainly she attempted to enter, but the heat drove her back.

Now dashing tears from her face, she raced across the graveled driveway toward the gates, where the guardhouse was located. No sign of life existed within the building and some instinct of survival slowed her pace to a careful creep. Out of breath and heaving from exertion, she nervously checked within.

Small puffs of white vapor colored the glass. She darted from one window to another. Her cloak drawn tightly around her body, hoping it would camouflage her from sight.

Satisfied, Jemima entered through the heavy, wooden front door and moved toward the phone she spied on the floor. Her eyes darting here and there she dialed, listening to the rotary motor as it returned to the proper position. Time was short and if *they* came back, she needed to have shared the message.

The phone rang once. Twice. With a brrping sound it connected.

"Hello?" A male answered and she felt a warm flush of relief at the voice. A voice she knew well.

"The manor has been breached. The girl child taken." The words erupted and her hand trembled.

"On our way." The click of the receiver being replaced echoed loudly in the stillness of the room.

Copper. She smelled copper.

Her stomach soured, knowing it meant more deaths. Jemima looked around for the gun—a gun with deadly, holy water-infused copper bullets—she knew was hidden somewhere in the room. A gun she couldn't find. *No divine intervention exists here*, she thought.

Hopefully *they* didn't remain. Feeding. If they were still here, that's what they would be doing. She found a corner and scrunched down, hiding from sight.

Crouched low, she tried to stay as still as possible, listening for sounds of the vehicles she knew would be coming. She dug her fingers into the flesh of her arms; remaining aware enough to stop before drawing blood. That would surely bring them out. Jemima dragged the cloak around her to capture the warmth, yet there was little to be found.

The sounds of engines roused her from the corner of the room. Jemima inched toward the window, the lead of the old glass distorting her view, hearing raised voices she knew Mistress Cressida had arrived.

Jemima retreated. Remained hidden from the woman because if she knew, all may well be lost. From the shadowed room she listened to the conversation...

"It smells like Estersham." The Mistress' eyes closed. "If it is, we have a problem." She turned once more, her face set and eyes now glacial in intensity. "James?"

The man nodded as if he knew what was to come.

"If I take those steps, I cannot return. Another must stand in my place." Her voice hardened while her eyes glittered in the dim light, piercing in their intensity.

Then the Mistress' voice called out in the near silence. "You and yours have been my loyal servants for so many years. I took an oath to protect you long ago. I renewed it with marriage and births, over and over. Now, my home and yours have been breached and this child taken from us. The girl child, who will be the hope and salvation of our kind, was ripped from the bosom of our nest. I will repay your loyalty and I will get her back." The words of power rippled in the night and licked at Jemima's skin.

Available in Ebook
books2read.com/BloodBride-Nix

Direct Autographed Copy
https://bit.ly/TBB-Nix

Also by Imogene Pitt

Warriors of the Elector

- Star of Ishtar
- Starline
- Starfire
- Star of the Fleet
- Starburst
- The Star of Eternity

The Star of Ishtar & Starline - Print

Starfire & Star of the Fleet - Print

Starburst & The Star of Eternity - Print

Blood Secrets (Re-releasing 2020)

- The Blood Bride
- The Illuminated Witch
- The Sorcerer's Touch

House Secrets (a Blood Secrets Continuation)

- As Dawn Breaks (Forthcoming)

The Search Duology

- Miss Elspeth's Desire
- Miss Isabelle's Craving

Reunion Trilogy

- War's End
- The Assassin

- Executing Justice

The Reunion Trilogy in Paperback

Sex Love & Aliens

- Tangled Webs
- False Webs
- Covert Webs

21st Testing Protocol

- Cyborg: Redux
- Children Of A Greater Evil
- When Evil Came To Stay (Forthcoming)
- Finis: The War To End All Wars (Forthcoming)

Celtic Cupid Trilogy

- Blame The Wine
- A Stranger's Embrace
- Revenge On Cupid

The Celtic Cupid Trilogy in Paperback

Zombieology

- The Reset (2018)
- I Dream of Zombies (2019)
- The Six Million Dollar Zombie (2020)

Knights of Pleasure

- Silken Knights (Forthcoming)

Single Titles

The Chocolate Affair (also in Print)

Falling In Love Again (Previously A Sapphire For Karina)

BioCybe (also in Print)

Hesparia's Tears (also in Print)

Tomorrow's Promise

A Bar In Paris (also in Print)

Inheritance Of The Blood (also in Print)

The Plan

Loving Memories (also in Print)

Hero of Heartbreak Hill (also in Print)

Raspberry Dreams (Forthcoming)

Non Fiction

Self Publishing: Absolute Beginners Guide (With Suzi Love)

Written as Ciara Cave

25 Curated Ways To Get Rid Of Telemarketers

Book Signings for Absolute Beginners

About the Author

Imogene is published in a range of romance genres including Paranormal, Science Fiction and Contemporary. She is mainly published in the UK and USA.

In 2010, Imogene Nix (the pen name not Imogene herself) was born. Imogene sat down and worked tirelessly for 3 months culminating in the book Starline, which became the first in a trilogy titled, "Warriors of the Elector." Since then she's had over 30 titles published and is now focusing on hybridising herself - with a mixture of traditionally published and self-published works.

In fact, she's taking control of many of her back catalogue books, which are slowly re-releasing as self-published titles.

Imogene is a member of a range of professional organisations world wide, and believes in the mantra of mentoring and paying it forward and is actively involved in mentorship (through NaNoWrimo and her vlog: In The Chair With Imogene Nix) and tutoring of new and upcoming authors.

In her spare time she loves to drink coffee, wine & eat chocolate and is parenting her spoiled dog and a ferocious cat along with her husband and 2 human daughters and looks forward to weekends away with her husband in their caravan "The Seven Year Hitch!" Do look forward to her caravan romance at some point!

To Contact Imogene

www.imogenenix.net
imogene@imogenenix.net

facebook.com/ImogeneNix
twitter.com/ImogeneNix
instagram.com/ImogeneNix